INTO NOWHERE

#

J M CLOSE

For my number one fan

BELFAST

February: 1997

Katey Doyle was driving too fast. She knew it. But with the boys running late for school she was going to be late for work. Which was not good. It would give that bitch, Mrs Miller, another opportunity to have a crack at her. Crabbie old cow.

The morning had not got off to a good start. No surprises there. Monday mornings in the Doyle household were never good. This one had been particularly bad. It was about to get infinitely worse.

It was all down to Daniel, of course. What was she going to do with that boy? What he needed was a good kick up the jacksie from his father. Not that this was likely to happen anytime soon.

So, this morning Daniel had refused to get out of bed. Exasperated, she had snatched back the covers and hauled him, yelling and kicking, from the mattress. He had retaliated by locking himself in the bathroom, and she'd had to force the door to get him out.

He then got himself ready for school with studied sluggishness. Sat eating his breakfast with all the gusto of a geriatric tortoise.

At fifteen minutes to nine Katey snapped. The half - eaten bowl of cornflakes went into the sink, followed by the near-full glass of orange juice.

She frog-marched Daniel to the car, thrust him onto the back seat with his brother Darren, made him belt up, and set off for school.

Now she drove down the hill to the crossroads, happy to see the traffic lights were on green. Had they been on red then the next two sets of lights would also have been against her, making her later still.

A sudden commotion erupted from the back seat. She lifted her eyes to the rear-view mirror. The boys were fighting.

'He's got my book!' wailed Darren.

Through the mirror she could see Daniel smiling at her. Winding her up. The boy was pure evil. Just like his father. 'Stop messing about you two!' she ordered.

'Mum he's tearing it!'

She glanced backwards over the seat. Daniel had hold of his brother's schoolbook and was pulling at it. Attempting to tear it in two.

'Daniel stop it!' she yelled. 'Give him back his book! Now!'

She returned her attention to the road. Her eyes widened in alarm. The lights ahead had changed from green to red and were now so close she had little chance of stopping. For a brief moment she considered driving through them, then her mother's instinct kicked in and her foot slammed down on the brakes.

It was too late. She sucked in a deep breath as, tyres screeching in protest, the car skidded into the junction. She had a fleeting impression of something huge bearing down on her. Then a tremendous impact hit the car, and everything went black.

SCOTLAND

October: 1998

The small, brick-built, toilet block was forty metres from the water's edge. It stood at the back of the car park, up against the trees that screened off the small fishing loch. It was a men-only toilet, which pretty much summed up the politics of the club. Female anglers were not welcome at Tannside.

At a little after midnight on a cloudy, moonless, night the building should have been deserted. It wasn't. The normally closed door stood ajar. The long, slit windows around the top of the walls glowed with light. Gathered inside the building were three men.

The first was standing just inside the doorway. He was pointing a Browning service revolver at a second man who stood against the wall, his wrists bound and gaffer tape covering his mouth. Sick with fear, the bound man's eyes darted frantically around the poorly lit interior of the toilet block. Searching for answers they were never going to find.

Between the gunman and the bound man was the third member of the small group. He stood just inside one of the open cubicles. His left foot was up on the toilet seat as he tied up the laces of the trainers he had just slipped onto his feet.

The light spilling from the building was attracting an

audience. Through the open door, a steady armada of insects invaded the small structure. Like tiny, guided missiles, they arrowed straight for the caged lamp set in the centre of the ceiling. Circled it excitedly in a growing cloud. Unaware of the drama taking place below.

'You going to be all night?' asked the man with the gun.

'Sorry,' offered trainer man, finally straightening his back.

'Bring him outside,' ordered the gunman. 'Turn off the light!'

As the bound man was led outside, strange keening and hooting sounds echoed dully from his sealed mouth. He was shaking violently, unable to contain his terror.

'Dirty bastard's shat himself,' observed trainer man, sniffing with disgust.

By the light from a torch, the small procession crossed the darkened car park. Behind them, in the sky above the trees, low clouds reflected the orange glow of the road lamps along the nearby highway. Ahead of them, looking out across the water, was nothing but blackness.

They walked past the dark shape of a car. Seconds later they came to a second vehicle that sat facing the loch. The gunman pulled open the driver's door and motioned with his head. 'Get in!' he told the prisoner.

The bound man shook his head. Refused to move. A savage blow to the stomach doubled him over. He was forcibly pushed down into the driving seat then his legs were lifted inside. The gunman held out the weapon to his accomplice.

'Here, kneecap him. Both knees. Then one in the head.'

Trainer man stared nervously at the gun. He shook his head. 'I can't do that!'

The other sighed. 'Look, I'm not asking you, I'm telling you! One of us has to do it, you know that. If I kill him that would make you a witness. So then I would have to kill you as well, making the whole exercise pretty bloody pointless. Here,' he thrust the gun into his companion's hand. 'Just get on with it! I promise I won't watch.' He turned his back. Stood gazing out across the dark water.

For long seconds the only sound to be heard was the muffled whimpering of the bound man. Then two gunshots rang out producing a muffled scream. The scream was quickly cut off by a third shot.

The gunman turned around. He looked into the car then retrieved his revolver. 'That wasn't too hard was it?' He studied his companion. 'You've never killed anyone before, have you?'

Trainer man shook his head. He stared at the dead man, horrified at what he had done. Suddenly he threw up, spraying vomit into the lap of the seated victim.

'Useless,' sighed the gunman. He walked around the car, winding down the windows. Then he leaned across the dead man, released the handbrake, and closed the door.'

'Come on,' he gripped the door pillar and reached for the steering wheel. 'Get back there and start pushing.' Together the two men pushed the vehicle towards the water's edge. On the slight incline it quickly picked up speed. Moments later the front wheels went over the edge of the low bank. The car went nose down into the water, then stopped. It teetered on the edge, momentarily hung up on the coping stones. But a final heave sent it sliding to the bottom of the deep loch, leaving a trail of bubbles in its wake.

'Job done,' said the gunman. He turned and headed back to the other car. 'Let's get out of here before some fanatic turns up with his fishing tackle. Close the gate will you.'

He started up the car and drove out of the carpark. Trainer man followed. He closed and re-bolted the access gate then climbed into the front passenger seat. The driver switched on the lights and headed back down the narrow lane. Minutes later they were turning onto the A75, heading for the M6 and the South.

PORTSMOUTH

June: 2014

The girl in the orange, shower-proof, jacket lowered the mobile phone onto her lap. She gazed ahead seeing nothing, her expression a troubled mix of concern and bewilderment.

Pamela Wharton was watching her. The girl had been repeatedly making a series of calls using single touch dialling. Calls that were obviously going unanswered. With each failure to get through, the girl became more agitated. Now she looked close to tears.

The teacher sighed. These kids, and their phones. She climbed to her feet. Moved a little unsteadily across the swaying lounge and sat down beside the girl. 'Are you alright, Rozalind?'

'I can't get through, Miss,' the girl told her. 'I've tried home! My mum's mobile! My dad's! Even my brother's? No one is answering my calls. Or texts.'

'Perhaps you can't make calls from the ferry?'

'But you can, Miss! We're close to land. I called my friend's home, just to see. Her mum answered.'

'Tell you what, I'll try with my phone shall I? Show me your home number.'

The girl held up her phone, the number on the screen. Pamela called the number. The ring tone went on for a while and then the answer-machine kicked in.

'Could they be out somewhere? Doing a bit of shopping before picking you up?' she asked the girl.

Rozalind shook her head. 'I don't think so. Dad never goes anywhere, these days. Mum might be shopping, but she always takes her phone with her.'

'What about your brother?'

'He works at Bertram's garden centre on Saturdays, for extra pocket money.'

'Does he have his phone on while he's working?'

'Usually! But he is not answering, either.'

Pamela looked up the garden centre and called the number. She spoke to the manager, explained who she was, and asked if Tony Carroll was in work.

'Tony hasn't turned in this morning,' he told her. 'Occasionally he takes a Saturday off, so we haven't chased him.'

She thanked him and closed the call. It was worrying. She could understand why the girl was becoming upset. But it was much too early to hit the panic button.

'Try not to worry,' she advised. 'We always think the worst when this kind of thing happens, but there's usually a simple explanation. We'll try calling again when we get to Portsmouth. Shouldn't be long now.'

Pamela stayed in the seat next to the girl until they docked. There wasn't much she could do to help. But she could, at least, provide a reassuring presence.

Thirty minutes later, the coach carrying the pupils pulled out of the Portsmouth ferry terminal. During the time it took to cover the seventy-three miles to the school in Dorchester, several attempts were made to get through to

Rozalind's parents. They all met with failure.

Pamela brought the problem to the attention of headmaster Paul Howarth. Paul decided there was nothing to be done until they reached the school. He was sure the girl's parents would be there.

They were not. The parents of the other children had arrived in force to collect sons and daughters, and hear all about the trip. But there was no one there from Rozalind's family.

By now the girl was in a state of near panic. Howarth decided to take her home in his car. Pamela Wharton sat beside her on the back seat. It took twenty minutes to reach the Carroll house. The detached property lay on the northern edge of the town. One of six executive homes built on the site of a former smallholding.

'Do you have a key?' asked Pamela as they pulled into the empty drive. The girl shook her head. The car stopped. Rozalind immediately jumped out. She ran to the front door, the teacher right behind her. The door stood slightly ajar. Two pints of milk rested on the tiled doorstep. The girl glanced backwards. Threw a quizzical expression at the teacher then pushed her way into the house.

'Wait Rozalind!' But the girl was already running down the hall, calling for her parents. Pamela caught up with her in the kitchen.

'Anyone home!' called out Howarth, following them into the house. His words were greeted by silence. 'You two stay here,' he ordered. Unlocking the back door, he went out into the garden. Took a quick look around. There was no one out there. Through the garage window he could see the family car sitting inside the small building.

Back in the house he checked the lounge. It was expensively furnished. A wide, leather, three-piece suite rested on a deep pile carpet. A huge, wall-mounted, TV hung on a chimney breast above what was once a stone fireplace. In one corner, a display cabinet showed off a collection of Lladro figurines. A quick glance around confirmed that there was no one in the room.

Crossing the hallway, he entered the dining room. There was no one in there either, but the table was set for three people. Breakfast dishes, cereals, and utensils sat on the oak table-top, waiting to be used. Thoughts of the ill-fated Mary Celeste crept, unbidden, into the man's head.

He climbed the stairs. Stepped onto a long landing. The first door led into a small bedroom. The girl's room. All pink furnishings, and boy-band posters on the wall. The neatly made bed, unused since she left for Normandy three days ago.

The master bedroom was on the front of the house. The bed had been slept in. The duvet turned back on either side as though the occupants had simply climbed out. Sitting on the bedside cabinets, each side of the bed, were two mobile phones. After a knock and a polite 'hello!' he entered the en-suite bathroom. No one in there.

He found the boy's bedroom. An electric guitar leaned against the wall next to an orange-coloured amplifier. The duvet had been thrown back off the bed. A mobile phone and I-Pad sat on a bedside table.

The next room was a study. It held a desk, made of light oak, on which sat an expensive-looking laptop. A printer and a laminator sat inside a corner cabinet.

Two rooms left. The one next to the boy's bedroom

was a tiled bathroom-toilet containing a built-in shower cubical. The room on the front of the house was an empty guest room. It held an unmade double bed and an oaken, free-standing, wardrobe.

Howarth returned downstairs. In the kitchen he found the girl sitting at a small round table made of black glass and stainless steel. Her face was pinched, and white with worry. He looked at the teacher. Shook his head and handed over the car keys. 'Put her back in the car,' he said softly. 'Stay with her. Something's not right here! I'm calling the police.'

DUTTON

Monday: Week 1.

There was a time, recalled Terry Dutton, when buying a light bulb was a relatively easy task. You only needed to know two things. The required wattage, and whether you wanted clear or pearl – which was slightly frosted – glass. Everything else about light bulbs was the same.

Things had certainly changed. Now he surveyed a bewildering array of bulbs, stacked along several shelves. Wondered if a degree course in light bulb technology might not have been a good idea, before setting off for the supermarket.

A five-minute consultation with a supervisor as confused as himself, did nothing to help. Happily, however, the instore cleaner seemed to know his onions – and his light bulbs – and kindly guided Dutton through the intricacies of modern lampology. Sorted at last, Dutton took his purchases back to the office. He kept the receipt. Just in case.

Now, standing on his desk, he fitted a new bulb into the dangling, empty, socket. When he reached the bit that required use of two hands, he was not at all surprised to hear the telephone, down by his feet, begin to ring.

He ignored it. Seconds later there was a brief knock on the door and Jo, his receptionist, walked in.

'If you are thinking of hanging yourself,' she quipped

brightly, 'that wire will never take your weight. Also, you have a visitor. A young lady!'

Some inflection of the word 'young' prompted a question. 'How young?' he asked, completing his task and climbing down from the desk.

'Teens-ish?'

'Has she an appointment?'

'Does she need one? What else are you doing besides changing light bulbs?' Lippy, too, is Jo.

'Who is she?'

'Roz Carroll.'

The name sounded familiar. Dutton wracked his brains. Then he remembered.

'Do you mean Rozalind Carroll?'

Jo stared at him. Her mouth dropped open. A hand came up to cover it. 'God, I didn't think! It was the Roz that threw me.' Her face took on the tragic look. The voice turned motherly. 'Oh that poor girl! You'll just have to see her!'

She was right, he decided. He would. 'Two minutes,' he told her. 'Give me two minutes, then wheel her in!'

Rozalind Carroll had made no attempt to hide her youth. Her face was free of make-up. The auburn hair attractively blown into a frizzy halo. She wore a dark green, blazer-style, jacket over a simple white t-shirt, with black fashion jeans, ruined by the compulsory frayed slits. Around her neck hung a chain carrying a small gold Ankh. She sat in Dutton's office on a plastic chair, looking remarkably cool and composed.

'Coffee, dear?' asked Jo, still in motherly mode.

'No thank you,' The girl's voice was strong, but still

youthful. 'Do you have a smoothie?' she asked.

Jo blinked. 'We have orange juice. With bits.'

The girl hesitated. Then decided it would be good manners to accept.

'Yes please.'

While they waited for the orange juice to arrive Dutton tried some small talk. Never easy with teenagers. They speak a different language than the rest of us. Live on a different planet.

'So, what do I call you?' he asked. 'Is it Rozalind or Roz?'

'Roz please. Everyone calls me Roz now. I prefer it. People don't associate with the name.'

He nodded sympathetically. 'Not nice is it? People gawping at you like you have two heads.'

'It's gross. But it doesn't happen so much now. I'm older. I've changed.'

Jo appeared with the juice. She set it down on the front edge of the desk then left them alone. The girl reached out. Lifted the glass. Sipped it experimentally. Satisfied, she took a longer drink. When she saw him watching she blushed slightly.

'Some of them are a bit sugary,' she explained. 'Too much sugar is not good for you.'

Unconsciously he drew in his stomach.

'Ok Roz, how can I help you?'

She took a deep breath. Looked him directly in the eye. 'I want you to find my family,' she said.

Now, while the words were not totally unexpected, they were, nonetheless, the very last words he had wanted to hear.

It was six years since the Carrolls had vanished, leaving

behind their daughter. A nationwide police operation, launched at the time, had turned up nothing.

Even now, several years on, the mystery was no closer to being solved than on the day it happened. All anyone knew was that at some point during a short, balmy, summer's night, Mr and Mrs Michael Carroll and their teenage son, Anthony, had simply vanished into nowhere.

According to the press, the police had found no evidence of a break-in at the house. No signs of a struggle. No enemies waiting in the wings to do the family harm. No indication that anyone in the family was involved in any criminal activity. In fact, apart from being much better off than most folk, which in itself can bring you to the attention of the wrong kind of people, the Carrolls were outstandingly ordinary.

The head of the house, Michael Carroll, had built up a successful coaching business. His fleet of luxury touring buses travelled, and still travel, the length and breadth of the British Isles. Carrying, for the most part, American and Japanese tourists.

The business had made Carroll a wealthy man. When he sold the Company to a National carrier, he became even wealthier. He also became something of a recluse. Idly, Dutton wondered if all that wealth now belonged to the young woman sitting before him.

In the years since the Carrolls vanished, the bulk of the family's money remained, untouched. Their bank accounts not drawn upon – with one exception. Local Social Services had been given legal access to a fund the parents had set aside to kick-start the careers of their children when they reached maturity. This was done to off-set the cost of bringing up Rozalind, who was taken into Council care.

But with the rest of the Carroll fortune still sitting in the bank, it seemed that whatever the disappearance of the family had been about, it had not been about money. Nor, apparently, about anything else that the police could put their finger on.

Roz was the child who had been left behind. Simply because, by pure chance, she had been out of the country on that fateful night. Now she was searching for answers, and Dutton could empathise with that. The problem was, she was looking to him to find these answers, and he was fairly sure he would not be able to do this.

'How old are you now Roz if you don't mind my asking?'

'Eighteen. Yesterday.'

Eighteen years old, he thought. Legally an adult. 'Have you spoken to the police?'

'They've had years,' she stated, simply, 'and found nothing. I think they have given up. So, I came here. They say you're good at finding people.'

This was true. But the people Dutton searched for were usually alive. The living tended to leave a trail. Dead people, like dead snails, did not; and according to the noises coming out of Winfrith headquarters, Dorset police believed the Carrolls to be dead. Dutton was inclined to agree with them.

He felt a sudden pang of sympathy for the girl. Would have loved to help her. But she was only just eighteen. A teenager. There were people out there who had been caring for her these past years. Regardless of her new status in law, they would still be protective of her. They would almost certainly take great exception to someone like himself filling her head with hope. Taking her money for a search that would, in all likelihood, prove futile. He smiled sadly. Shook his head gently.

'I'm sorry Roz. I can't help you with this.'

Her face fell. 'I have money,' she offered. 'I can pay!'

'Roz, this is not about money. Or about how good anyone is at finding people. You said it yourself. The police have had six years, and when it comes to finding people, they are the best. I know this because I used to be one of them.

They have more resources, more technology, and more manpower at their disposal than any private investigator. So, if they cannot find the answers you are looking for, then the chances are they are not there to be found. I'm sorry. I would only be filling you with false hope if I agreed to help you, and I'm not prepared to do that.'

For a long moment she studied the glass of juice in her hand. Fought back her disappointment. Then she stood up. Placed the unfinished drink on the desk and nodded.

'Thank you for seeing me,' she said quietly. She turned and walked to the door. Pulled it open, stopped, then looked back. 'You think I'm still a kid, don't you? With some fanciful notion that they are out there somewhere, waiting for me to find them. Well that is not what I think at all.

But I have waited for six years to be able to do something about that night, Mister Dutton. So, with or without your help, I am going to find out what happened to my parents and brother. Even if it takes forever and costs every penny I have.'

'What do you think happened to them?' he asked.

She stared at him solemnly. 'I think they are dead! And if they are, I want to know why!'

'What makes you think they are dead?'

'Because they wouldn't have gone off without me. Well, my mum wouldn't. Nor would my brother. I don't know about dad – he's not my real dad, anyway.'

She threw him a long, final, look. Hoping he would change his mind. When he didn't, she turned and walked from the office. He caught the echo of her footsteps along the corridor. Heard her murmur a polite 'thank you' to Jo. Then she was gone.

2

'Well?' asked Jo, appearing around the door.

'She wants me to find her family.'

'And you turned her down?'

'I had to. I'm a private investigator, not a medium.'

'You think they're dead?'

'Everyone thinks they are dead. Even she thinks they are dead.'

'She's very disappointed.'

'I know. But she is young. She'll get over it.'

'Will she?'

Dutton checked his watch. He climbed to his feet and slipped on his jacket. 'I'm going out,' he told her. 'I'll be back after lunch. Jack Rigby is coming in this afternoon to pay his dues. He's bringing a case of Pinot Noir, as a thank-you. You can take a couple of bottles home if you like.'

Her face lit up. 'Oh, thanks boss! I'll take back what I told my husband about you being tight.'

'Yeah, right!'

Going down the back stairs and out through the yard, he climbed into his car. Drove to the golf club. He went to the range and took it out on a bucketful of balls. He wasn't feeling too good about himself.

Trouble was, he knew something of what the girl had

gone through. He too had endured the tragedy of losing a loved one under sudden and inexplicable circumstances. But in his case, there was tangible, if false, evidence that the person was dead. In Roz's experience she had lost the whole of her family without ever finding out what had happened to them. Or why?

His heart went out to her. But he still felt it would be a mistake to give her false hope. Her parents were almost certainly dead. Her brother too – unless he was the one who killed them, and he was sure the police would have considered this possibility.

After lunch at the club he went back to the office, feeling like he had just stolen Christmas from Tiny Tim. In the mid-afternoon Jack Rigby came and went, leaving behind his money and the Pinot Noir. Dutton loved customers like Jack.

By four-thirty he decided to call it a day. Leaving Jo to lock up, he left his Weymouth office and drove home to Portland.

By the time he arrived home he had talked himself into changing his mind. For one thing, he found the Carroll case far too intriguing to pass up on. For another, he did not want Roz to be ripped off by some hack private investigator she went out and found on the internet.

Alex, his wife, would not be home until after seven. She was working full-time at her flower shop in Swanage whilst Jenny, her manager, was on maternity leave. Pouring himself a glass of wine he sat down, opened up his laptop, and began reading up on the Carroll story.

According to Roz, Michael Carroll was not the children's natural father. Yet he found nothing in any of the newspaper reports to suggest this. Perhaps he had legally adopted them?

The night the family disappeared, Roz had been in Normandy on a half-term school trip. Visiting the D-Day landing beaches, and the war graves of the fallen. Visiting Bayeux, too. To view the Tapestry that depicted the battle of Hastings and the events leading up to it, from a French perspective. After three days away, she returned home to find her parents and her brother had vanished.

The lead journalist on the story, Mark Addyman, had done a series of follow-up articles on Rozalind. She had been taken into care by the local authority. Then fostered by Pamela Wharton, the teacher who had looked after her since the day her parents disappeared.

There had been some legal issues. Social Services had wanted to sell the family home to pay for the girl's upbringing – something they were entitled to do, apparently, whenever parents died, and their orphaned children were taken into care. But because the Carrolls were not demonstrably deceased, the application was refused.

As a compromise the judge allowed the family home to be rented out by the Council. He also gave limited access to one of the Carroll's bank accounts, to minimise the burden of Roz's care on the taxpayer.

As with all big mysteries, the disappearance of the Carrolls filled the newspapers for a few weeks. But as progress stalled and speculation dried up, the story began to take a back seat.

In one article Addyman had hinted at a terrorist link to the family. But the police had quickly dismissed this notion. 'None of the Carrolls had been involved in Irish politics,' insisted DCI Rudman who was leading the investigation. 'And any speculation of this kind is both misplaced and unhelpful.'

At just after six-o-clock Dutton's phone rang three times. Then it stopped. Alex was leaving the shop. It was time to start preparing dinner.

After dinner they took Lucy, their Lakeland Terrier, for a walk. Then they both settled down for the evening with a glass of Rigby's Pinot Noir.

'You'll never guess who I had in the office this morning,' he began.

'Roz Carroll,' she answered without taking her eyes from the book she was reading.

He stared at her. Then the penny dropped. 'You've been talking to Jo?' he accused.

'No,' she looked up and smiled. 'I've been talking to Roz. She came to the shop.'

'Did she, now?'

'She wants me to ask you to reconsider.'

'Well she's persistent, I'll give her that. So, go on then,' he urged.

'Go on what?'

'Ask me to reconsider!'

She shook her head. 'I'm not falling for that. You've already changed your mind. It's written all over your face.'

'I'll tell her you talked me into it.'

'Like I could! But I'm glad you've decided to help her. Right now, everyone is telling her to put it all behind her. Get on with her life. The trouble is, she can't.'

Dutton nodded. 'The problem here is that this won't be like any missing person enquiry I've ever done. If they are dead – and the police certainly think they are – then I'll be sticking my nose into what is, effectively, a murder enquiry. And there are so many reasons why that is not a good idea.'

'Then tell her that. She'll understand. But if you only just poke around a little, at least she'll feel that someone is listening to her.'

'Okay, I'll poke around a little. See where it leads. To nowhere, I should think.' he added.

'You may be right,' she told him. 'But if there is anything out there to be found, you are the one to find it.'

'God, I wish I had your confidence in me.'

3

Tuesday: Week 1

The next morning Dutton called Bonner House school. Asked to speak to Pamela Wharton. The teacher was not available, so he left his number. Then he called the Dorset Free Herald. Asked if reporter Mark Addyman was still working there. He was put on hold.'

'Addyman!' the journalist announced when he came on the phone.

'Mark, it's Terry Dutton. Abacus Investigations. I'm calling about an article you wrote some time ago when you were covering the Carroll story.' He could almost hear the man's ears prick up.

'Oh yes? So what is a private investigator doing, looking at the Carrolls?'

'Just a bit of research!'

'Research? Right! So which article was this?'

'The one in which you hinted at a possible terrorist angle. The one that was rubbished by the police.'

'You mean Rudders!'

'That's him, Rudman. Were you just speculating? Or did something put the idea into your head?'

The journalist thought for a moment. 'I know the one you mean,' he said at last. 'Give me five minutes to find the file and I'll call you back. Let me have me your email address?' Dutton gave out his address and put down the phone. It rang immediately.

'I have a Pamela Wharton on for you,' Jo told him. 'I'll put her through.'

'Ms Wharton?'

'Mrs!' corrected the teacher, 'what can I do for you Mr Dutton?'

'I was wondering if we could meet up. Lunchtime, perhaps? I need to speak to you about Roz Carroll.'

'Roz?' A note of caution entered her voice. 'I hope she hasn't been bothering you.'

'Not bothering me, no. But she has asked me to look into her parents' disappearance.'

'Oh, I'm sorry to hear that. Just lately Roz has become a little fixated on past events. I'll have a word with her. Tell her she must leave you alone.'

'I'd rather you didn't, Mrs Wharton. Not until we've had a chat, anyway.'

There was a silence, then, 'I really can't think of anything we need to talk about Mr Dutton? But if you feel you have something to say, my lunch break is twelve-fifteen until one. I'll be free then. Just ask for me at the school office.' She put the phone down.

'Thank you,' said Dutton, speaking to himself. When the phone rang again it was Addyman.

'I've emailed you a photograph,' he began. 'Take a look at it.'

Dutton searched out the email. Opened the attached photograph. It was a black and white shot of three men standing outside the entrance to a building.

'What am I looking at?'

'That was taken in front of the old cop shop on Weymouth Avenue. Five days after the Carrolls vanished.

The guy in front, with the belly, is Rudman. The two behind him are DI Jim Penny and DS Alan Badell, with the moustache.'

'Right?'

'Now, look at the glass door behind them. Just over Badell's left shoulder. See it?'

'I see it.'

'There's someone behind the door. Inside the building. See him?'

Dutton studied the photograph. There was a figure behind the door. He was peering through the glass at the three policemen outside. 'Dark coat, white shirt, dark tie?' he said.

'That's him. It's not best of shots, with the reflection on the glass, and all. But it's good enough to make him out. His name is Gerald Dawson. He worked for the security service.'

'Really?'

'Really. At first, I had him down as Met. I thought Rudders had called in some help. So I got one of our editorial nerds to enhance the photo and put it out on a forum we use. I got a hit from a reporter in Dublin.'

'Dublin?'

'Turns out Dawson was a spook. Ran the Northern Ireland desk. I called the reporter for more info. He told me that back in the nineties Dawson was a field officer in Ulster.

Seems that while he was over there, he was *outed* by a journalist who was investigating loyalist assassination teams. Accused of setting up targets for them. It was never proved, but they had to pull him out in a hurry.'

'Why was he in Dorchester?'

'My question exactly. I figured if he was sniffing around the Carroll case, then he was there for a good reason. But when I asked, I got shot down.'

'Did you follow it up?'

'Nah! Moved on. Settled for a human-interest story on the girl. The whole thing was something of a seven-day wonder, anyway.'

'Alright! Well thanks Mark, I owe you one.'

'You do! And I hope you remember that, if and when your 'research' turns up anything interesting.'

'Tell me about Rudman,' said Dutton. 'Do you think he'll talk to me?'

'Doubt it! They cremated him last August. Prostate cancer.'

'What about his team? Penny and Badell?'

'Penny's a DCI now. It's gone to his head. I doubt he'll even take your call. Badell is your best bet. He's off the force. Shattered his hip in a motorcycle accident. Left him walking with a limp. He runs a motorbike repair business in Lyme Regis, now. Lives over the shop. You'll find him there most days.'

'Do you have an address?'

'It's called Silver Wheels. Look it up.'

'Thanks Mark. You've been very helpful.'

Dutton ended the call. It wasn't much but it was a starting point. He checked his watch. There was plenty of time before his lunchtime date, but he decided to set off for Dorchester, anyway. With only a forty-five-minute window, he didn't want to risk being late.'

4

Dutton thumbed the bellpush. When he heard the click, he pushed through the door into the school. Found himself in a spacious entrance hall with walls covered by student artwork. To the right was a table. Behind it sat a boy and a girl. The boy was reading a comic. The girl was doing something with an e-tablet.

He crossed to the reception window. Peered through, into the school office. A lady wearing a smart plaid suit and a pink rollneck sweater, came to the window.

'Can I help you?' There was a touch of the Penelope Keith about her.

'I'm Terry Dutton,' he announced. 'To see Pamela Wharton. She is expecting me.'

'Ah, yes.' She looked over his shoulder. Called out to the tablet girl. 'Chloe, take this gentleman to the print room please.'

He followed the girl along a maze of corridors and into a library. A few students sat around reading or studying. Others were busy at computers. At the far end of the long room was a closed door. The girl knocked, then opened the door and ushered him through.

The cluttered room was dominated by two, large, photocopiers. Around the walls hung shelves filled with reams of paper, boxes of toner, files, books, and a large assortment of other things that looked like they belonged there. Seated in a corner, drinking from a beaker and working on a newspaper crossword, was a woman he assumed was Pamela Wharton.

He turned to thank Chloe for delivering him safely, but she had already returned to her tablet. The teacher climbed to her feet. She was late thirties to early forties, bespectacled, and wearing a grey skirt, white blouse, and grey cardigan. Mrs Wharton looked exactly as he had expected a schoolteacher to look.

She offered a small, cool, handshake. Indicated a second chair. 'Sit down if you like. Can I get you a coffee, or a tea?'

'No, I'm fine, thank you,' he said, lowering himself onto the chair.

She returned to her seat. Put aside the crossword and looked at him keenly.

'So, what can I do for you, Mr Dutton?'

'As I said,' he began, 'Roz came to my office yesterday. She asked me to find out what had happened to her family. I turned her down. Mainly because I didn't think I could succeed where the police had failed. I still feel that way. But on reflection, I think turning her down might have been a mistake.'

Her eyes turned wary. 'So, what are you saying? That you will now take on this search, even though you expect to fail?' Her voice hardened. 'And how much is that going to cost her?'

He leaned forward in the chair. 'Look, I don't want Roz's money. That's not what I'm about. But yesterday she made it pretty clear that if I didn't help her, then she will go somewhere else. This is her choice, of course, but not all the agencies out there are as ethical as they might be. I would not want to see her being ripped off – as I am sure you wouldn't.'

She looked at him searchingly for a moment, and then relaxed slightly.

'No, I would not,' she stated. 'So, what is it you intend to do?'

He told her.

Forty minutes later he sat in the car, outside the Wharton family home. Pamela had called Roz and told her he was on his way there. Roz was in town with friends. But she would make her way home and meet him there. It was a pleasant day. The autumn sun was shining. He opened the window a little and sat reading the local paper.

Eventually a small, yellow, Ford Ka passed by. It turned into the Wharton driveway. He saw Roz Carroll step from the car. She locked the car then looked in his direction. Closing the window he left the newspaper on the passenger seat, climbed out, and followed her into the house. Five minutes later they sat in the lounge, drinking ground coffee.

'What made you change your mind?' she asked. 'Was it your wife?'

'Yes and no,' he smiled. 'She certainly caused me to do some deep thinking. But I was also concerned you might end up hiring some rubbish investigator. Someone who would rob you blind, and still come up with nothing.'

'How do I know you won't rob me blind?' she asked with a faint smile.

'Because if I did, my wife would kill me.'

The smile widened. 'She probably would.'

'Ok Roz!' he began. 'Here's the deal. I will give you two weeks – at no cost. Two weeks, during which I will take a close look into the circumstances surrounding the disappearance of your mum, dad, and brother. If, after this time, I find there is nowhere I can go with the investigation I will tell you so, and that will be game over. Do you understand?'

'Yes.' she nodded.

'But if I do find something worth pursuing, I will tell you what I have found. Then, any decision about where we take it from there will be down to you, and to the police. You, because from that point onward it will start to cost you money. The police, because your family's disappearance is still a live investigation. This means that anything I turn up will have to be passed on to them. I must also warn you that in a case like this, the police will almost certainly tell me to butt out!'

'Can they do that?'

'If I am interfering with an ongoing investigation, yes they can.'

She digested this. 'But if you do carry on, how much will it cost?'

'A lot of money. I don't come cheap. But we can talk about that, if and when.'

She awarded him a huge smile. 'Thank you, Mr Dutton. For changing your mind.'

'That's alright: and the name, by the way, is Terry.'

'So, when do we start, Terry?'

'*We* don't,' he told her pointedly. '*I* am going to start right now with a lot of questions. Questions you will almost certainly have been asked already, by the police. But since they are not likely to share their case notes with me, I will have to start from scratch. That okay with you?'

'Ask away!' she told him.

An hour later Dutton had learned a lot about the Carroll family. None of it giving any hint or indication of the reason behind their strange disappearance. But he had discovered a few things he had not known before.

Four years separated Roz from her older brother Tony. Both were born to Emma and Anthony Roebuck who, according to Roz's mother, had met in a disco, fallen in love, and married a year later.

Roz couldn't remember her biological father. She was only a year old when he died of a brain haemorrhage. But she did remember being a bridesmaid at her mother's wedding to Michael Carroll, for whom her mum had been working as a part-time secretary.

Once they were married, Carroll had adopted both children. Her new father had been strict, but generous. He had bestowed upon his wife and children a lifestyle that was infinitely more comfortable than anything they had been used to.

They had wanted for nothing. Roz and her brother attended the best schools. Both had great futures mapped out ahead of them. Tony should have taken his A-levels the year he disappeared. Roz, also, was academically bright, and destined to follow in her brother's footsteps.

Dutton questioned the girl closely about her father. Despite being successful in business, in his private life Michael Carroll was somewhat shy and introverted. He had no extended family. No close friends that Roz had ever heard him speak of. If he went out socially at all, it was with his wife and family.

After selling his business, he retired. Spent most of his time shut inside his study listening to music. Tapping away on the computer keyboard. When asked what he was doing, he would jokingly say he was writing his memoirs.

There was talk at one time of buying a property in France. Or Spain. Somewhere that Michael and Emma Carroll could retire to when the children left home. But as far as Roz knew, this had never gone beyond the talking stage.

By the time he was finished, Dutton had heard nothing that might, conceivably, have triggered whatever had occurred that fateful night.

'Would you like to see the house?' she asked.

'Is that possible?'

'I don't see why not. I go there sometimes, just to look at it. The Shaws live there now. But I don't think they'll mind. When would you like to go?'

'Will they be in now?'

'He might be. He's retired.' She grabbed her phone. Keyed in a number. 'I'll check.'

5

They turned into Mayflower Close. Pulled into the kerb outside number seven. 'Nice place,' he remarked.

'I loved it here,' she told him, looking at the house. 'But I couldn't live here now.'

'Are you coming in?'

'No thank you. I haven't been in there since that day.'

He left her in the car. Walked up the block-paved driveway to the house. The front door opened before he reached it. A man in his sixties, wearing brown cords and a blue rugby shirt, peered out at him.

'Mr Shaw?'

'Come in Mr Dutton.' The man did not offer a handshake. Just waved him through. 'Roz not coming in?'

'Too many ghosts, I think!'

'I can understand that. Sometimes she drives up here in that little car of hers. Sits out there, looking at the house. Then she drives off. We found it a bit creepy at first. But we've got used to it now.'

They were in a long, wide, hallway with three doors. One at the far end of the hall facing the front door. The other two set one on either side of the hallway. Immediately to his left, an open staircase ascended to the upper storey.

'Roz tells me you are retired,' said Dutton. 'What sort

of work did you do?'

'I worked in local government.'

The clipped response implied that this was all the information Dutton was about to get. He changed tack. 'And you're wife?'

'Still working. She works in a library.' The man studied his visitor closely. 'So, what's this all about? Are you looking to re-open the case? Succeed where the police failed?'

Dutton smiled. 'This is just a preliminary exercise, Mister Shaw. To see if there is anything left to pursue. For Roz's sake - not mine.'

'Well if it helps, be my guest. Nose around all you want. But I'll come with you if you don't mind. No offence mister Dutton, but these days it doesn't do to let strangers wander around your home on their own.'

Dutton didn't spend much time in any of the rooms. There was no point. Whatever had happened here, happened years ago. Any pertinent evidence would be long gone. He was mainly interested in the lay-out of the house.

One of two things had occurred here, he decided. Either the Carrolls had walked down those stairs, out the front door, and gone off to god only knows where? Or they had been brought down by someone, forced into a vehicle, and taken away.

The first scenario was improbable. Their night clothes were missing. Who goes off in their nightwear? They also left behind the family car, which begs the question what did they use for transport? Certainly not a local taxi, the police would have checked that. Then, as Roz herself had said, what kind of mother would go off and leave a twelve year old daughter behind? The answer had to be no one. Which just left abduction.

The front door was the most likely exit point. Just a few feet from the bottom of the stairs. It would be too easy to get three people outside and into a waiting vehicle. The houses were built on an outwardly curved crescent, across from open fields. With the front not overlooked, whatever had happened that night was unlikely to have been witnessed by any neighbour.

Shaw allowed Dutton to explore the back garden on his own. Like the front of the house, the rear was not overlooked. A detached garage, alongside the main building, spilled over into the rear garden.

At the bottom of a long, tidy lawn stood a wooden shed, padlocked shut. He peered through the window. Inside were the usual lawnmower and other gardening implements. Poignantly hanging on the back wall of the shed were two rusting bicycles. A boy's and a girl's.

Returning to the patio he studied the rear of the house. A sliding door gave access to the dining room. The door had a standard, three-lever lock with multiple locking points. The sturdy kitchen door was also well secured.

The police had found no sign of a break-in. Yet someone had got in, despite good security and an alarm. Perhaps someone had let them in?

When he had seen enough, Dutton thanked Shaw. He returned to the car. Found Roz listening to a CD of *Les Misérables*.

'I hope you don't mind,' she said. 'I love this. We went to see it in London. On stage.'

'One of my wife's favourites,' he told her. 'I'm more into heavy metal, myself.'

'What's heavy metal?'

Dutton suddenly felt old.

Back at the Wharton house he sat drinking tea. Roz was encased in a deep armchair, sipping on a smoothie.

'Are you going to stay on living here?' he asked.

She shrugged. 'I could do! Pamela and Eddie said I could. I should have gone to Uni last year, but I felt I'd had enough of school. I could still go. I want to be a writer. A degree in creative writing would be useful.'

'Then go. University is nothing like school. You'll enjoy it. I had a ball there.'

'Truth is, I'm a bit nervous about going away. Even though I know it's not going to happen, I have this niggling little worry that they might come back for me and I won't be here. Stupid, isn't it?'

'Not really,' he told her. 'When someone dies, they are usually cremated or buried. Either way the people who loved them know they are dead. They can accept that they are gone forever. But when someone just disappears, it becomes so much more difficult for those left behind to come to terms with the idea that they will never see them again.'

'I suppose,' she agreed, sadly.

Dutton changed the subject. 'Do you have any photographs of your family?'

Without a word she climbed to her feet and went up to her room. Minutes later she was back. Handed him a sheet of photographic paper. It held a colour print she had just run off.

'That isn't the original,' she told him. 'The police took that away. But I took a picture of it with my phone, before I left for France. I'd never been away from home on my own before. It was my way of taking them with me. This is the only picture I have of the four of us. Dad didn't like having his picture taken.'

Dutton wondered about that. In his experience as a policeman, people who did not like having their photograph taken usually had good reason not to. He studied the photograph she had given him. The family were walking down a wide avenue with palm trees. Parents on the outside, the children between them. The sun was shining. They all smiled happily.

'I was eleven there,' she told him. 'We went to Disneyland the year before they disappeared. This was taken by one of the Disney photographers. Mum bought it off him.'

'What about other family photographs? Your mum and dad's wedding photographs?'

'Don't know,' she shrugged. 'They told me to take what I wanted from the house before they cleared it out, but I never did. I couldn't go back in there.'

'Well this will do,' he told her, folding the sheet and tucking it into his pocket. 'I understand your father was from Ireland?'

'Northern Ireland.'

'Whereabouts?'

'He was from a place called Ballymena.'

'Do you know anything about his background? His politics? Was he Catholic? Protestant?'

'I don't know. I don't think he was religious at all. We never went to church or anything, and he never talked about Ireland. The only reason I know where he came from is because they played a piece of music on the radio one day, when we were going to school. The DJ said the

the tune was called Ballymena, and mum said that was where dad came from.'

'Did your father ever talk about any relatives he had? Or friends.'

'He had no relatives. The police checked. I don't know about friends. He never seemed to go anywhere that he could make friends.'

'Which Disneyland did you go to?'

'Orlando.'

'Then your father had a passport?'

'I suppose?'

'Do you know where it is?'

She shrugged. 'All the stuff was taken from the house when it was rented out. The police had already taken some things away. The rest were put in storage somewhere. The Council sorted it all out. I suppose all that stuff belongs to me now?'

'Well it certainly doesn't belong to the council. You should get in touch with them. There could be things in there you would like to keep. Important things.'

'That's what Pamela keeps saying,' she nodded.

6

Helen Shaw drove up onto the brick drive. She pointed the activator and pressed the button. The garage doors swung open and she drove inside. Switching off the ignition she grabbed her handbag and the half full shopping bag. Climbed out and locked the car. Then she closed the garage door and entered the house.

'Good day?' Shaw asked his wife by way of greeting.

'Quiet,' she smiled, an old librarian joke. 'You?'

'Had visitors,' he told her.

'Oh?'

'Roz was here.'

'Roz? Did she come inside?'

'She didn't. But her friend did. He was a private investigator, no less.'

His wife sank down into a chair and kicked off her shoes. 'Don't tell me he's looking into the Carrolls?'

'He's thinking about it. A preliminary exercise, he called it. Wanted to look around the house. Get the feel of the place. Personally, I think he's wasting his time.'

She looked at him thoughtfully. 'Perhaps we should call Mr Dawson?'

'D'you think that's necessary? It's been a long time!'

'I know. But he did say to call him if anybody came asking questions.'

'But that was years ago. Roz is not going to be in any danger now, is she? Not after all this time.'

'Probably not. But that's for him to decide, not us. Go on, give him a call.'

Obediently he climbed to his feet. Went through into the hallway. He came back with the telephone and the phonebook. Pulled a card out of the book and studied it. 'It's probably been deleted by now.'

'You could be right. But at least we'll have tried?'

The number wasn't deleted. On the fourth ring the call was answered.

'Mr Dawson? It's Frank Shaw,' he began, 'From Mayflower Close, Dorchester.'

'Yes, I remember. Go on Mr Shaw!'

Shaw described the visit of the private investigator.

'And he was with the girl, you say?' Dawson asked.

'She was with him. But she stayed in the car. She never comes in here.'

'Ok we'll check him out. Thank you for calling.' The call was abruptly ended.

'Man of few words, that one,' commented Shaw, slipping the card back into the book.

'Better that he knows, though!' Helen told him. 'Then it won't be our fault if there is anything amiss.'

7

Wednesday: Week 1

Dutton was in the office for nine-o-clock. He spent some time writing up his notes, then he prepared a couple of accounts that had to be sent out.

At nine-thirty he opened up a subscription search engine, used by journalists and private investigators. He typed in the name Michael Carroll, followed by Ballymena, Northern Ireland. He pressed search.

Amongst other things, the data base held UK electoral registers going back to year dot. It took around five minutes to find what he wanted. A Michael Thomas Carroll lived at number twenty-one Manser Steeet, Ballymena, until October 1998. According to Roz, her father had started up his coaching business in 1999 so the timing looked good. He called Roz.

'Did your father have a middle name?'

'Thomas,' she told him. 'My mum would call him Michael Thomas when he was in trouble.'

'I think I just found his old address in Ballymena.'

'Is that good?'

'It's a start,' he told her.

Next he googled 'Silver Wheels' and came up with an address. He wrote it down and left the office. Dutton spent the next hour with his accountant, then he took an early break. After lunch at the yacht club he called Jo. Told her he was going to Lyme Regis, and then home.

It took him an hour to get to the resort town and find the repair shop. Silver Wheels was located in what might once have been a large barn, or storehouse, tucked away in a private yard behind Silver Street. The ground floor of the building was a well-equipped repair workshop. An exterior metal staircase, attached to the side wall, led up to living quarters above.

There was a small office inside the workshop. In there, seated at a chaotic desk was a bearded man. He was on the phone. He signalled he wouldn't be long, then carried on talking to someone about gaskets.

'Can I help you?' he asked when he finally put down the phone.

'Alan Badell?'

'That's me.'

'Terry Dutton,' he handed out a card

Badell studied the card. 'Private Investigator, eh? So, what can I do for you Terry?'

'I'm taking a look at the Carroll disappearance.' If Dutton had expected this announcement to take the man by surprise, he would have been disappointed.

'Well good luck with that,' Badell offered. 'Hope you have more success than we did.'

'Actually, I was hoping you'd be able to help out. Fill in a few blanks for me.'

Badell grinned. 'You mean you want me to tell you how far the investigation went?'

'Something like that.'

'Why are you doing this?'

'For Roz.'

'Roz?'

'Rozalind Carroll.'

'Oh, the girl? How is she doing?'

'She's eighteen now and looking for answers.'

Badell nodded. 'Can't say I blame her. Well I wasn't on the case for long, you know. I had my accident a few months into it.'

'Anything you might remember could be useful?' Dutton told him.

'Brew?' offered Badell.

'Coffee please. Milk and one sugar – heaped.'

The mechanic pointed to a grubby-looking chair. 'Have a pew, while you're waiting.' He limped away. Dutton checked the seat for oil. Finding none, he sat down. Waited. Some minutes later Badell was back with two mugs. He handed one over.

'I've heard of you' he said. 'You are an ex-copper, like me. Why did you pack it in?'

Dutton shrugged. 'My father died. Left me a lot of money. Too much money to carry on working.'

'Lucky you! I was all but kicked out of the force. But I suppose it was my own fault.'

'What happened?'

'The night before the accident I'd been out on a bender. Riding into work the next morning I hit a sharp left-hander. I'd taken that bend a thousand times without a problem. But this time, some pillock had spilled diesel fuel all over the road surface and I lost it. Went into the side of an HGV coming the other way.

A Devonshire traffic cop was the first to respond. He decided it would be a good idea to breathalyse me while we waited for the ambulance to arrive. I told him I was job, but he did it anyway. Found I was still over the limit.

The accident shattered my hip. Broke my leg in two places. They pinned it all together as best they could, but it healed up shorter than it had been. That was game over for me. Who needs a copper with a gammy leg?

Then, to make matters worse, I was prosecuted for driving under the influence. Got a fifty-pound fine and a one-year ban. The conviction meant I couldn't even apply for a civvy job with the force. So that was it. Game over! I suppose I should be grateful they let me keep my pension.'

'You seem to be doing alright' offered Dutton.

'You're looking at five years hard work here. But it's coming along.'

'So, the Carrolls?' Dutton reminded him gently.

Badell told him everything he remembered about the case. The investigation had been thorough, and wide-ranging. Conducted by an experienced team of officers. Yet despite all their efforts they just ran into blind alley after blind alley.

'I don't know if there have been any developments since I left the force,' he added. 'If there have been, they don't seem to have been much use. As far as I can see they are still nowhere with it.'

'What about the Irish angle? Anything in that?'

'Rudders certainly thought there was. He went to his grave swearing the paramilitaries were involved.'

'Yet when the press speculated about that, he stated there was no terrorist connection.'

'He was told to say that. Besides, we had no proof. The Ulster police looked into Carroll's background and found zilch. The man was about as political as a rich tea biscuit. Even MI5 dismissed the notion.'

'Who brought them into it?'

'I don't know. Might have been Rudders. He had this bee in his bonnet. During the Ulster troubles, back in the eighties and nineties, if any member of the paramilitaries broke the rules, they would be punished.

Kneecapping was used for minor offences. But if someone grassed, or undermined the organisation in any way, they would be shot in the head and buried where they would never be found. These victims became known as '*The disappeared*'. Rudman thought this might be what happened to the Carrolls.'

'And what do you think?'

Badell shrugged. 'Perhaps he was right, who knows? But whatever happened, they're almost certainly dead.'

Dutton finished his drink. He climbed to his feet. Thanked Badell for the coffee and the information.

'What are you going to do?' asked the mechanic.

'I think I'm with Rudman on this,' Dutton told him. 'The Irish link was never really checked out. Perhaps it should be. Michael Carroll came from Ballymena, in Country Antrim. I've never been to Northern Ireland. Perhaps it's time I went.'

'Well, good luck with that one, too!' offered Badell.

Dutton headed back to the car. As he climbed in, the ex-policeman called out to him. 'Better watch yourself over there, mate! Some of them are still at war with us.'

8

Thursday: Week 1

Next morning, Dutton was on the seven-o-clock flight from Bristol to Belfast. By eight-thirty he was through Belfast International airport, making his way to car hire. He picked up a Corsa, with satnav, and entered the address he was looking for.

Leaving the airport, he took the A26 heading north. Half an hour brought him into Ballymena. Staying on the same road, he drove through the town until he was directed to head off towards the shopping district.

Manser Street ran close to Thomas Street and the Fairhill shopping centre. It was made up mostly of older terraced houses with a mix of shops and small businesses. Driving along, he passed a hairdresser's, a baker's, and a print shop, sitting amongst the houses.

He pulled into an empty bay with an hour's free parking. In front of him was a white van. It belonged to two men who were fitting new UPVC windows to a house. Leaving the car, he walked back down to number twenty-one. Rang the doorbell.

A woman came to the door. Early twenties. She had dark hair, green eyes, and a hawkish face. In the crook of her left arm sat a small boy. He had a dirty face and was sucking a dummy. The boy stared curiously at Dutton through large, wide, eyes, the same colour as the woman's.

She eyed him with suspicion. 'Are you the po-lice?' she asked.

He held up a business card that she didn't even look at. 'I'm a private investigator,' he told her. 'I'm looking for information on someone who used to live here. His name is Michael Carroll. Does the name mean anything to you?'

'Never heard of him,' she answered in her strong Ulster accent. 'When was he here?'

'Until the end of 1998. Then he left for England.'

'Is he dead?'

'Why do you ask that?'

She shrugged. 'I thought maybe you was looking for relatives - for the will and all that. Isn't that what you people do?'

'No, it's nothing like that. He's gone missing. His family are trying to find him.'

She shook her head. 'Ninety-eight? Long before our time. We've only been here three years.'

'How about your neighbours? Any of them been here long enough to have known him?'

Another shake of the head. 'Wouldn't think so. These are all to-let houses now. Folk come and go all the time. You can try the newsagents up the street,' she pointed up the road. 'Been there forever, so they have.'

Dutton thanked her. He turned and stepped off the kerb, glancing up and down the street. Four or five houses back, a white car was pulling into a parking bay. There was no other traffic approaching from either direction. He stepped out into the road, walking diagonally towards the newsagent's shop.

He had walked maybe twenty yards. Had almost reached the far kerb when an urgent shout rang out.

'Watch out mister!'

He turned. Silently bearing down on him, on the wrong side of the road, was the white car. Even as he saw it, he knew it was going to hit him. Reflexively he bent his knees and sprang upwards

The car hit his legs, scooping him up onto the bonnet. His head and shoulder hit the windscreen then he was sliding off the bonnet, over the passenger-side wing.

As he left the vehicle, the wing mirror gave him a parting blow to the back of his head. Luckily, the mirror was collapsible, or the impact on his skull might have been worse. Dutton crashed down heavily onto the road and the car sped away.

BALLINGER

9

Thursday: Week 1

John Ballinger checked his watch. It was eight a.m. London time. He peered out the window as the plane taxied to the terminal. As always, he found himself slightly overawed by the sheer size of Heathrow. The juddering, trundling, journey from the touch-down point to the terminal felt to take forever.

At last the aircraft arrived at the gate and stopped. The engines wound down. This was the signal for most of his fellow passengers to unfasten their seat belts and climb to their feet. Pull down their hand luggage then clutter up the aisles as they waited for the doors to open.

Ballinger stayed in his seat. He waited until most of the passengers had disembarked, before standing and reaching down his holdall. He placed it on the seat and checked to see that the small, black, plastic case was still inside, and then he zipped it shut. He made his way down the now deserted aisle, thanked the South African cabin crew, and exited the aircraft.

Arriving at immigration he joined the slow-moving queue. When he was passed through, he moved on to baggage claim, but he didn't linger there. Strolling down the long hall he headed for the exits. He entered the red channel and placed the bag on the table.

'Good morning,' he said, cheerfully.

The customs officer didn't do cheerful. He gave a curt nod. 'Name?'

'John Ballinger.'

'Is this all the luggage you are carrying?'

Ballinger nodded.

'What are you declaring?'

Ballinger opened the bag and removed the black, plastic, case. He placed it flat on the table next to the holdall and unlocked it. He opened it up. Lying snugly inside were twenty, one-ounce, gold Kruger Rands. From his pocket Ballinger removed the importation documents and handed them over.

The Officer checked the paperwork then did a quick count of the contents of the case.

'You work for McClean?' he asked.

Ballinger shook his head. 'Private courier,' he said.

'Hmm!' The paperwork was re-folded, returned to the envelope, and handed back. The case was re-locked and put back in the hold-all.

'Anything else?'

Ballinger shook his head. The Customs man waved him through. He followed the passageway through to arrivals. At the front of the waiting crowd was a young woman. She held a white card, bearing his name.

'I'm Ballinger!' he told her.

She switched on a welcoming smile. 'Follow me please, Mr Ballinger.'

The car was an Audi. She unlocked the doors and climbed into the driver's seat. He placed the holdall into the foot-well and climbed in beside her. The interior of the car smelled of the perfume she wore.

'Nice car!' he commented. 'Yours?'

'The Company's.'

'McClean's?'

She shook her head. 'VIP Transit. We're a glorified private hire company. Specialise in ferrying VIPs in and out of London.'

'VIP? Ballinger was impressed. Business class air travel. Now the VIP treatment! A man could get used to such a life- style.

The journey up the M40 to Oxford was a good hour's drive. As they travelled along, Ballinger discovered that his driver was studying medicine at the London University Hospital. Driving VIPs around in her spare time mitigated the city's high cost of living.

'I thought junior doctors worked long hours,' he remarked. 'How do you find time to do this?'

'I'm not a doctor,' she told him. 'Not yet. Next year I'll be a doctor. Always assuming I pass my finals.'

'You'll pass,' he told her. 'If you really want to.'

She flashed him a smile. 'Thank you for the vote of confidence.

Bullion dealers R. L. McClean occupied a small, single storey, industrial unit in the Botley area of Oxford. The driver dropped him outside the main doors of the building, and Ballinger offered up a twenty-pound tip. She accepted it graciously and drove away, giving him a small wave. He made his way inside.

'Mr McClean, please' he asked the receptionist. 'He's expecting me.'

'What name is it?'

'Ballinger!'

A phone call brought McClean through to reception.

He was around five feet tall and almost as wide. His suit was Saville Row, but with his bulk Rory McClean was never going to look smart.

The dealer offered a handshake 'Good trip, Ballinger?'

'Very good. Thank you for the business class - and the VIP car.'

'You are welcome. But it is not just about your comfort. It's about security too. About minimising risk.' He turned back to the door from which he had emerged. 'Come on then, let's get this business sorted.'

Ballinger followed McClean into a corridor. At the far end of the passageway were two doors. The one on the left bore a polished brass plate carrying the word Office. The door on the right was unmarked. It was sheathed in stainless steel and secured by an electronic lock.

McClean held a card to the pad and the lock clicked open. The bullion dealer led the way into the room, switching on the lights as he did. The door closed and locked itself, automatically.

They were in a windowless room. Twenty feet square, with a concrete floor. Against the far wall stood two, large, steel safes. The only other furniture in the room was a metal desk with a chair placed either side. McClean sat down behind the desk. He motioned to the other chair. 'Sit down Ballinger. Any problems?'

Ballinger sat down with his back to the door. He unfastened the bag and removed the case. 'None,' he assured the dealer. 'Sailed through customs.' He placed the case on the table and opened it up.

McClean eyed the contents and whistled. 'Beautiful,' he breathed. Reaching in he took out one of the coins and carefully studied both sides through a jeweller's eye glass.

'If you ever want to invest your money Ballinger,' he advised, 'invest in some of these little beauties – '

There was a sudden crash, somewhere out in the corridor. Then the raised voice of the receptionist could be heard, followed by the sound of running feet.

Moments later, someone banged on the door.

'What the hell – ?' growled McClean.

There was a loud thud as something struck the door. This was followed by a second blow. Then a third. The fourth blow split the doorframe. The fifth finally smashed open the door. Men began to pour into the room.

Ballinger was on his feet in an instant. His foot shot out and the leading man went down, his legs kicked from under him. He just managed to plant a pile-driver on the nose of the second attacker before being overwhelmed and forced to the floor.

Handcuffs were snapped onto his wrists. He was dragged to his feet, receiving a vicious kidney punch that took his breath away. On the other side of the table McClean was shouting and cursing loudly as he was forcibly restrained by two more men.

A woman swept into the room. She was tall, blond, and anywhere between thirty and fifty. She wore a long black raincoat over a dark blue, pinstriped, trouser suit. In her hand was an open wallet displaying a warrant card. She thrust it towards Ballinger, then McClean.

'Customs and Excise!' she snapped. 'You're nicked! Both of you.'

Ballinger gave McClean a questioning look. The dealer looked away.

They were put into separate cars and taken to St. Aldates

police station. Processed, and then locked up in separate cells. Two hours later Ballinger heard someone unlocking the cell door. A sergeant entered, with two constables.

'On your feet!' he was ordered.

One of the constables stepped forward as Ballinger climbed stiffly from the bunk. The officer was carrying a pair of handcuffs.

'You don't need those,' Ballinger complained.

'Yes we do,' said the sergeant. 'I don't want any of my lads in hospital.'

'I was defending myself!'

'So are we!' The sergeant stood beside the cell door. 'Take him along,' he instructed his men once the cuffs were in place.

'Where am I going?' asked Ballinger.

'Interview room. Your Customs friends want to talk to you.'

'Not without my lawyer.'

'You won't need a brief. They are not going to question you. They're going to charge you.

10

Friday. Week 1

He was awake when they brought his breakfast. The pain in his back was receding. Down to a dull ache if he didn't move too much.

When he had eaten the food, Ballinger pushed the tray to one side. He looked around and swung his legs off the bed. The cell was a little minimalistic, but he'd spent nights in worst places. All the same, he would hate to serve time in prison. He had been here, what, twenty hours? Already he was going stir crazy.

An hour later he heard footsteps on the other side of the door. The lock was turned, and the door swung open. The custody sergeant walked in.

'Your brief's here.' The policeman collected the empty tray as Maggie De Havilland stepped into the cell. 'Give a shout when you've done,' he told the lawyer, pulling the door closed behind him.

Ballinger raised his hand in a small wave to his sister. She wore a dark grey suit over a white, roll-neck jumper. Around her throat hung a string of polished onyx stones that had once belonged to their mother. Her long ginger hair was tied up in a bun. The thick-framed spectacles she wore, her courtroom spectacles, rested on a small turned-up nose that was surrounded by freckles – also a legacy of their mother.

She regarded him over her glasses. She did not look overly pleased to see him.

'Thanks for rushing over, Mags!' he offered.

'I was in court yesterday! I do have a paying job, you know?'

Ballinger nodded. He patted the bunk. She checked it for stains then sat down beside him. Gave him one of her looks.

'How is his Lordship?' he asked. Maggie was married to High Court Judge, Donald De Havilland.

'Donald is fine. So, what have you got yourself into this time?'

Ballinger told her about the courier job he had taken, carrying Kruger Rands for bullion dealer McClean. Then about what had happened as he was handing over the coins.

She listened to his story then gave out an audible sigh. 'John, do you not think it's time you found a real job?' she asked. 'One where you don't spend your life consorting with chancers and lowlifes.'

'You mean like those people you spend most of your life defending,' he grinned. 'Anyway,' he added, 'I do have a job. I am a Security Consultant.'

'Guarding dodgy Kruger Rands?'

'They weren't dodgy. They were legally imported. Donald McClean is a respected bullion dealer – or so I thought.'

'Then why have you just spent the night in a police cell?'

'Diamonds,' he told her. 'Seems the coin tray had been moulded around a load of uncut diamonds.'

'Did you know this?'

'Don't be silly!' he told her.

'Have you been charged?'

'Yes. Conspiracy to handle. Conspiracy to evade excise duty. Oh, and assault.'

'Want to tell me about that?'

'I punched one of them in the face when they jumped us. Apparently, I broke his nose.'

She grimaced. 'You do know, don't you, that assaulting a Customs Officer ranks somewhere just below assaulting the Queen?'

'I didn't know he was a Customs Officer. I thought he was a villain. I thought they were all villains. Trying to steal the coins.'

'They didn't identify themselves?'

'Not to me, they didn't. Not until they'd knocked seven bells out of me.'

'Who was in charge?'

'An SPO called Linda Wormald.'

'And they definitely didn't identify themselves?'

'She did – after the others had battered down the door and charged in'

Maggie checked her watch. 'You're up before the magistrate at eleven thirty. Let's go through it again, frame by frame, so that I know exactly what we're up against.'

At ten-thirty Ballinger was back in the interview room. This time with his lawyer. Across from him sat Wormald and another plain-clothed customs officer.

'What has My client been charged with?' asked Maggie.

'I'm sure he's told you!'

'I want you to tell me SPO Wormald.'

'Conspiracy to handle stolen goods. Conspiracy to evade paying excise duty. Resisting arrest and causing actual bodily harm to a customs officer.'

Maggie pensively chewed her bottom lip before speaking. 'Yes, well the first two are untenable, as I'm sure you know. The diamonds, as I understand it, were secreted within the moulding of the coin tray. Mr Ballinger could not possibly have known they were in there. To get the DPP to bring him to trial on this, you will require evidence that shows he did know they were there. Do you have any such evidence?'

'We're working on it,' smiled Wormald.

'Has Mr McClean, implicated my client in any way?'

The Custom's officer gave a barely perceptible shake of the head. 'Not yet.'

'But you are working on it. It seems to me, SPO Wormald, that Mr Ballinger has no case to answer here. The fact is, he had no idea that he was carrying anything other than the Kruger Rands that he had been legally contracted to collect. Coins that he declared at the airport, along with the excise paperwork issued for them.

How could he possibly know what was secreted in the case moulding that was delivered to him in the lobby of the Peermont Hotel, as witnessed by reception staff. If you insist on putting him before the magistrate on these charges, you will have to put the South African Airlines pilot and crew up there with him. For they, too, played a part in transporting the diamonds to Mr McClean. Are you working on doing that, too?'

'There is still the matter of the assault!' Wormald said sourly. 'Your client resisted arrest and put one of my officers in hospital.'

De Havilland smiled. 'Yes, I heard about that! This would be one of those Customs Officers who burst into the room like a bunch of smash and grab thieves, without first identifying themselves. Am I right?'

'Procedures were followed.'

'SPO Wormald, the only time procedures were followed was when you and your team entered the reception area. After identifying yourselves to the receptionist, you demanded access to the rest of the building. When the receptionist refused your request and tried to call her employer, a member of your team smashed open the door leading into the corridor. Still ignoring the protestations of the receptionist, your men then broke down the strong-room door.

In fact, until the moment that you yourself entered that room, by which time the altercation was over, not one member of your team had identified himself as a customs officer.'

'This is nonsense. My officers identified themselves, both before and after they broke down the door.'

'You know that do you? You've seen the videos?'

The Custom's officer looked confused. 'Videos?'

The barrister leaned forward. 'Mr McClean is a Gold Merchant. Every square inch of his premises is covered by video cameras, with audio. Both inside, and outside the building.

I have just spoken to Mr McClean's office manager Peter Deeley. He has studied yesterday's videos in the presence of Mr McClean's lawyer. They clearly show that your people broke down the strong room door without any attempt to identify themselves.

Mr Ballinger naturally responded to this sudden and

violent incursion because he feared your men were criminals, there to steal the Kruger Rands. I'm afraid your men let you down, Ms Wormald. In their eagerness to make the collar, they blew it!'

Half an hour later Ballinger was turned loose on police bail, pending further enquiries.

'Thanks Mags, I owe you. Do you think they'll take it further?'

'Not unless they can prove that you knew about the diamonds: and they won't be able to do that, will they?'

'No!' he assured her. 'They will not.'

'Good! How will you get home from here?' she asked. 'Hitch-hike?'

'No don't do that. You'll end up in some kind of trouble again. I'll run you home. You can fill up my petrol tank on the way.'

'If you insist.'

'I do.'

11

Ballinger heard the phone ringing inside the house as he climbed from the car. He collected the bag of groceries and his holdall from the rear seat. Waved goodbye to his sister as she drove off. By the time he entered the house the phone had stopped ringing. He carried the bags into the kitchen.

Taking off his coat he hung it over the back of a chair. He took out his mobile phone. Frowned when he saw it was switched off – probably by the police when they took it from him. Now he pressed the on switch and left it on the table whilst he put away the groceries.

The phone came to life. Then it gave out a series of sharp beeps. He picked it up and checked the screen. He had eight missed calls. All from Alex, the wife of his friend Terry Dutton. He fast dialled the number. The call was answered immediately.'

'Sandy, thank God! I've been calling you for ages,' said the woman.

'Sorry Alex, I've been travelling back from Africa with my phone switched off,' he explained, half truthfully. 'What's wrong?'

'I'm in Antrim. Terry's in hospital here. He's had an accident.'

'What kind of accident?'

'He was hit by a car.'

'Jesus! How bad is he?'

'Concussion and leg injuries. They were a little worried yesterday. He kept on drifting in and out of consciousness. I haven't seen him yet, today, but I called the hospital this morning. He had a quiet night and he's a little better.'

'What was he doing in Antrim?'

'Working a case!'

'Where did they take him, the Area Hospital?'

'Yes – but look, you don't have to rush over here. That's not why I'm calling. I just wanted to let you know what had happened.'

'I'm coming anyway. I'll grab a flight and see you at the hospital this evening. That ok?'

'That's fine. Thank you, Sandy,' there was a hint of relief in her voice.

He had a quick shower then changed his clothes. Emptied the holdall and refilled it with clean t-shirts and underwear. Then he checked out flights to Ulster. There was nothing out of Bristol until tomorrow. He tried Exeter.

Ten minutes later he was in the car on his way to Yeovil. From there he headed south, towards the A30. He arrived at the airport in time to catch the last flight from Exeter to Belfast City Airport. By seven o clock he was heading North-West, out of Belfast.

It took thirty minutes to cover the twenty miles to the Antrim Area Hospital. He had called ahead so Alex was waiting for him, in the main reception. She walked him through to where Dutton lay.

'When did this happen?' he asked.

'Yesterday. I was out delivering orders and left my phone in the shop. When I got back there was a message to call the Ulster police. They told me Terry had been involved in an accident and was in hospital. They wouldn't give me any details, so I closed the shop, left Lucy with Jo at the office, and caught the first flight over here.'

'Do you know what happened?'

'Only than he was run down by a car. His head hit the windscreen, so they did a scan. There was no fracture, or bleed, but he was badly concussed. It caught his legs, too. They were cut and bruised, but nothing was broken. His shoulder was dislocated, but they reset that.'

'What do the police say?'

'Not much. The car didn't stop, so they are treating it as a hit and run.'

'What was he doing in Ballymena?'

'Working on a case. Digging up background on someone who went missing some years ago

When they arrived at the critical care unit, Dutton was no longer there. They were redirected to a general ward. There they found him sitting up in bed. He looked a mess. His forehead was one great bruise and he had two black eyes. But he attempted to smile when he saw them both.

'Hell's bells, I must be bad if they've sent for you,' he said, giving Ballinger a welcome nod.

'What happened?' asked Ballinger.

'Can't remember. Got a nasty crack on the head, so I'm told.

'Good job it was just your head,' grinned Ballinger. 'Anywhere else, it might have done some damage.'

'You're not wrong,' agreed Dutton. He turned to Alex. 'Have you told Jo what happened?'

'I have. She's holding the fort.'

'Where did this happen?' asked Ballinger.

'Manser Street, in Ballymena,' Alex told him.

'How did he get there?'

'He hired a car from the airport.'

'Hang on, hang on,' put in Dutton. '*He* is not dead yet! *He* can speak for himself!'

'I thought you couldn't remember what happened?' Ballinger reminded him.

'Yeah, well, I may not remember the accident, but I do remember arriving at the airport and picking up a car.' He turned to his wife. 'Did you get my laptop?'

Alex frowned. 'No! All I have are the things the hospital gave me, from your pockets. The police must have your laptop. I'll call them.'

Alex called the number she had been given by the police. The Traffic officer dealing with the accident was unavailable until tomorrow. She was told that any valuables left in the car would have been recovered by the road traffic officers on scene.

'I'll try again tomorrow,' she told the duty sergeant.

Ballinger stayed half an hour, then left the couple on their own, giving them some time together. He waited for Alex by the main entrance.

'How did you get here?' he asked when she caught him up.

'Taxi.'

'Where are you staying?'

'The Dunsilly hotel. Just outside Antrim.'

'That's where I'm heading. Come on, I'll run you back there.'

'Thank you for coming, Sandy,' she told him once they were in the car. 'It's really good of you.'

'He'd do the same for me. You both would. How long are you planning on staying here?'

'As long as it takes. Lucy will be fine, staying with Jo. The shop will have to remain closed for a while.' She turned to him. 'Listen Sandy, please don't feel you have to stay here on my account. I'm feeling better already, just from seeing him sitting up and chatting. Yesterday was so scary, though.'

'It must have been a shock?'

'It was. I barely slept last night.'

'When was the last time you had something to eat?'

'Breakfast.' She told him.

'What did you have?'

'Muesli.'

'Muesli?' he shook his head, sadly. 'Muesli is not breakfast? Muesli is a penance!'

'I wasn't very hungry.'

'Okay. Think you can manage dinner tonight?'

'I think so?'

'Good, because I'm starving, and I hate eating alone in hotels.

12

Saturday Week 1

The next morning Ballinger made his way to the dining room. Alex was already sitting at a table.

'How'd you sleep?' he asked.

'Better,' she told him.

'Good. Have you ordered?'

'Not yet. I was waiting for you.'

They had their breakfast. Ballinger was a 'full English' fan. Alex settled for cereal and eggs benedict. He was happy to see her eating something more substantial than grated cardboard.

'Did the hospital give you Terry's keys?'

She dipped into her handbag. Came out with a bunch of keys. Hanging from the main key ring was a car key with a car-hire tag.

'I don't think the police have the car,' he told her, pointing to the key. 'Or they'd have kept that.'

'You mean it's still out there? On the street?'

'Unless the car hire people picked it up? After breakfast try calling the police again. Ask them where the car is – or more importantly, the things from inside it. My guess is that since it wasn't actually involved in the accident, they might have just left it where it was.'

Thirty minutes later, Alex spoke to the traffic officer. He told her that nothing had been removed from the scene of the accident, but the hire company had been contacted and asked to collect the car, and its contents.

Ballinger called the hire company. The girl he spoke to knew nothing about any accident, or police request. As far as she was aware the car was still out on hire. He finished his coffee and picked up the keys.

'I'll go and collect his things,' he said. 'You want to come?'

She shook her head. 'I'll wait here.'

'Then I'll see you later.'

He left the hotel. Took the Ballymena road. Thirty minutes later he turned into Manser Street. It wasn't difficult to find the car. The rear window carried a car hire sticker, the front several parking tickets. He pulled in behind it.

Climbing from the car he pressed the button on the key fob to unlock the Corsa. He saw immediately that the front passenger window had been smashed. He opened the door. Looked inside. Unsurprisingly there was no laptop. He moved on to the boot. In the space where a spare wheel would once have been stored sat a holdall, containing Dutton's clothes. Still no laptop.

'You looking for something?'

Ballinger looked up at the man asking the question. Around fifty, he was wearing grey coveralls under a black anorak. He was carrying a hammer.

'I'm a friend of the guy who was knocked down here the other day.'

The man nodded at the broken window. 'Thieving bastards!' he remarked. 'Bad enough the poor man's in the hospital. But to rob him as well – ?' He stuck out a hand.

'Joe Keegan. Working on the house there,' he waved the hammer at a nearby property. 'How's yer man doing?'

'No serious damage,' Ballinger shook the beefy hand. 'Concussion and leg injuries, mainly. He'll be okay. Were you here when the accident happened?'

'So I was,' said Keegan. 'And I can tell you now, mister, that was no accident.'

'What d'you mean?' asked Ballinger

'I was upstairs fitting the frames. Your man came away from that house, a couple of doors down. He walked across the road and the next thing I see is this white car, coming up behind him. One of those hybrids, so it was. Running on electrics.

I shouted a warning and he looked round. But he had no chance. The car was right on top of him. He went up on the bonnet, bounced off the windscreen, and hit the road like a bag of sand. A wicked thing to see. The driver switched to petrol drive, then just took off. Left him lying there in the road.'

'Anyone else see it?'

'I don't think so,' he nodded towards a second workman who was collecting something from the back of the van, 'my mucker there had his back to the road. But, like I said, that was no accident. Your man had almost made it across. That driver had lots of room to pass. But he went straight at your man.'

'Did you tell all this to the police?'

'So I did! Fat lot of good that'll do. That car will turn up some place, burned out. Like they all do.'

'Did you see the driver?'

'Big fella, so he was. Didn't see his face, though. He was wearing one of those hoodies.'

Ballinger thanked the workman. He walked down to the house the man had indicated. Rang the bell. A young woman, in a dressing gown, opened the door.

'Yes?'

'I'm making enquiries about the guy who was knocked down here the other day. I believe he called to see you?'

She nodded. 'And you are?'

'I'm a friend of his. Would you mind telling me why he was here?'

'He was looking for someone who used to live here. Someone called Michael Carroll. I've never heard of the man. I told him to try the newsagent. Poor fellow must have been going over there when the car hit him. How is he?'

'He's been better.'

'Poor fellow,' she repeated. 'I hope he'll be alright.'

'Thanks.'

Ballinger crossed the road and walked to the newsagent's shop. Inside, sitting behind the counter, was an elderly man. He was reading the sports section of a newspaper. Ballinger introduced himself to the newsagent who was called Danny Reid. He gave the old man an update on Dutton's condition.

'He was on his way to see you when he was knocked down,' he told the newsagent. 'He was looking for information on someone called Michael Carroll. Used to live down the road there.'

'Number twenty-one, the Carrolls' nodded the man. 'Michael was born and raised there. I don't think he ever knew his daddy. He was long gone before the boy was out of nappies. Michael lived with his mother until she passed away. Then he left. Went to work in Scotland.'

'What was he like?'

'A quiet fellow. Never in any trouble.'

'Was he political?'

The man shook his head. 'Well, he was gay – which is about as political as you can get with some people around here. But he was a good Protestant lad, and generally kept himself to himself.'

Ballenger left his card with the newsagent. The man had no information that was of any help. But he did promise to call Ballinger if anyone else came asking about Carroll. Leaving Ballymena, he took the road down to Aldergrove airport. He entered the car hire office and placed the car keys on the counter.

'I called earlier. About the car you hired out to Terry Dutton. Is it you I spoke to?'

The girl admitted it was. She told him she had made enquiries and had learned that the police had indeed called yesterday, about the car. Unfortunately, no one had done anything about it.

'I wasn't in work the last two days,' she explained. 'They were short-handed and didn't have anyone to collect it. I'll make sure it's picked up today.'

'It's been broken into. Mr Dutton's laptop has been stolen. It's also covered in parking tickets, so I suggest you have it moved before it gets towed.'

'I'll sort it,' she promised.

'Good!' Ballinger turned to leave. As he pulled open the door he turned.

'Do you have a record of what time he picked up the car that morning?'

She consulted the computer. 'Eight-forty.'

'Thank you.'

Back at the hotel he carried Dutton's holdall to Alex's room.

'I called Terry,' she told him.

'How's he doing?'

'He sounded quite bright. Did you find his laptop?'

He shook his head. 'Stolen! The car was broken into.'

'Oh, great! That's all he needs.'

'Alex, this wasn't an accident. The witness I spoke to told me the car deliberately ran Terry down.'

Her eyes widened. 'Why would anyone do that?'

'Well, this is Ulster,' he reminded her. 'There are lots of secrets here. Things people would rather forget. Knocking on doors and asking about someone who has disappeared, might not be the smartest thing to do.

Having said that, however,' he went on, 'Terry had only been here for an hour. Not long enough to upset anyone. Who is this Michael Carroll he was asking about?'

'Carroll was a retired businessman. He disappeared, with his wife and son, six years ago. They were never found. Terry was looking into the disappearance for their daughter, Roz.'

Ballinger had not been living in Dorset when the Carroll story had broken. Alex filled him in on the details of the case. She explained how Terry had become involved, and how Carroll's background had brought him to Ballymena.

'So, either some local head case suddenly decided it would be fun to run down a total stranger,' he remarked, 'or Terry was targeted. If he was targeted, then it had to be by someone back in Dorchester. Someone who knew he was travelling to Ulster. How many people knew what he was working on?'

'Well, the girl of course. Her foster parents. Terry had spoken to a few other people, but I don't know who, or how many. You'd have to check his notes.'

'Where are they?'

'On his laptop. He writes them up every day, like clockwork. It's his police training.'

'So, without the laptop we're struggling?'

'They'll all be backed up, on his icloud account.'

'Do you have his password?'

'Yes, I do!'

'Okay, that's good! I'll check them out when I get home.' He looked at her seriously. 'You do know that Terry is not going to drop this, don't you? Especially now! This will tell him there is something here worth looking at. So as soon as he's up and about he'll back here, asking more questions.'

'I know.'

'Perhaps I should take a look at the people he spoke to before any more grief comes his way. Do you think he would mind?'

'He might if he knew,' she smiled. 'But if he doesn't ask, I won't tell him.'

13

Monday. Week 2

Monday morning. Ballinger took his leave of Alex. By Sunday evening it had become apparent that Dutton's condition was much improved. But his whole body had bloomed into a mass of painful bruises. Even the bruises had bruises on them.

He flew back to Exeter, and by lunchtime he was back home. He made himself a coffee then opened up his laptop. Using Dutton's password he downloaded the case notes from the iCloud account. Sat reading them whilst chewing on a sandwich from the airport.

The notes were pretty comprehensive. He was able to follow the trail from Dutton's first meeting with the Carroll girl, through to the interview with Alan Badell, the day before he left for Ulster.

Dutton had built up a sketchy profile of the Carrolls. He had spoken to Pamela Wharton, with whom the girl lived, and visited the Shaw house. Ballinger would get to these people later. First, he wanted to speak to Addyman, the journalist.

He called the number and introduced himself as a colleague of Dutton. The reporter was cagey at first. But when he heard what had happened, he became more attentive.

'Is Dutton alright?'

'Head injuries!' Ballinger told him, 'and a bit knocked about. But he'll live.'

'What do the police say?'

'Hit and run.'

'Bloody hell!'

'Did you know he was going to Ulster?' He asked the journalist.

'I knew he was thinking about it. He thought Carroll's Irish connections were worth looking into.'

'Did you tell anyone?'

'Come on Ballinger, I'm a journalist! Whatever it is that Dutton is up to, there's a story in there somewhere. You think I'd want to share that around?'

Ballinger didn't. 'Probably not.'

'He said he'd tip me off if he found anything, in exchange for the information I gave him.'

'Yes, I have the picture you sent him. I think it was this that sent him off to Ulster. Tell me, are you going to publish what I told you? About Dutton's accident?'

'Of course.'

'Do you think you could lay it on a bit? Make out he is more seriously injured than he actually is?'

'That would be lying.'

'What, are you telling me journalists don't lie? Anyway, you wouldn't be lying. You'd be speculating!'

'Okay! I suppose I could speculate. But not without knowing why.'

Ballinger paused a moment, unsure how much to tell the journalist. 'Strictly off the record, this might not have been an accident. He may have been targeted.'

'You're kidding?'

'The only people who knew he was going to Ulster are

here, in Dorset. I don't want whoever set him up to think Terry is going to bounce back from this anytime soon, or they might be tempted to have another go.'

'Alright, I get that. I'll put him on death's doorstep if it helps. But now you owe me, too'

'Then watch this space. If anything breaks, you'll be the first to know.'

Ending the call, Ballinger printed off copies of the photographs in Dutton's file. Security agent Gerald Dawson behind the glass door of the police station: the Carroll family in Disneyland: and Roz Carroll herself, caught on Dutton's office security camera.

He needed to speak to the Carroll girl. There were questions he could not ask Dutton. Questions that she might hold the answers to. When he called her number she answered immediately.

'Roz Carroll?' he asked.

'Yes!'

'You don't know me Miss Carroll, my name is John Ballinger. I am an associate of Terry Dutton.'

'Yes?'

'Terry is in hospital. Over in Ulster,'

There was a slight intake of breath from the girl. 'Why? What happened?'

'An accident. He was hit by a car. He's okay! And despite what you may read in tomorrow's papers, he should make a good recovery. But while Terry is out of action, I am looking into a few things for him. Is there somewhere we can meet?'

'What? Like, now?'

'Now would be as good a time as any.'

'How do I know you are who you say you are?'

'No problem! When we finish speaking, call Dutton's office. Talk to Jo, his receptionist. You've met her. She knows I'm a friend of Terry's. She'll vouch for me.'

'Okay!'

'So where would you like to meet?'

'McDonalds, Bridport Road.'

'See you there in an hour,' he told her, ending the call. Minutes later he was climbing into the car when his phone sounded. It was Dutton's office. 'Hi Jo!'

'Did you just arrange to meet the Carroll girl?'

'I did.'

'Okay! Just checking it was you. She says you are taking over the enquiry. Is this true?'

'Not quite! At the moment I am only interested in finding out why Terry almost got himself killed.'

'Alex says it wasn't an accident?'

'It's looking that way.'

'Then you be careful. We don't want any more accidents.

'I'm always careful Jo. By the way, tomorrow's local newspaper are going to exaggerate the seriousness of Terry's injuries. Just ignore the report. It's a smoke screen. He's doing alright, really.'

'Thanks, that's good to know.'

Ending the call, Ballinger set off for Dorchester.

14

He recognised the girl as she entered the car park. She reversed the car into a bay opposite from where he was sitting. Unhitching the seat belt, she spent a few seconds organising something, possibly her bag, on the passenger seat next to her. Then she climbed out and strode purposefully towards the restaurant. He slipped her photograph into his wallet and left the car. Followed her inside.

The place was not busy. Roz Carroll stood alone at the counter. She had just ordered an iced Smoothie. 'Add a regular latte to that will you,' he told the young man taking the order. He smiled at Roz and stuck out a hand. 'John Ballinger,' he introduced himself.

Tentatively she shook his hand. 'Hello,' she said.

'Grab a seat, I'll get these.'

She didn't argue. He paid for the drinks and carried them to the window table where Roz was now sitting, phone in hand. As he placed the drinks on the table his own phone began to vibrate. He went to take it from his pocket.

'Don't bother,' smiled the girl, holding up her phone. 'It's me. Jo gave me your number in case you were someone pretending to be you.'

'Do you feel threatened?'

She shook her head. 'No, but I've had problems with reporters in the past. You wouldn't believe the things they'll do to get past your guard. So now I like to make sure I know who I'm talking to.' She took a small sip at her drink. 'So, go on then, what's happened to Terry? Will he be alright? I feel awful, like it's all my fault! He wouldn't have gone there but for me.'

'He'll live,' Ballinger said the words lightly, to take the edge off her anxiety. 'He hit the windscreen with his head so they're keeping an eye on him for a few days. Don't blame yourself. These things happen. He could just as easily have been knocked down walking his dog.'

'Does his wife know?'

'She's with him now. She'll be staying there until he's allowed home. He will be ok you know?' he assured her.

The girl nodded but did not look any less concerned. She studied Ballinger appraisingly. 'What did you want to talk about?'

'I've been going through Terry's notes. There are some questions I need to ask. That okay?'

She nodded.

'First off, did Terry tell you he was going over to Northern Ireland?'

She shook her head. 'He called me, Wednesday morning. Said he had found my dad's old address in Ballymena. But he didn't say he was going there.'

'Did he mention any names? Anyone he seemed particularly interested in?'

She shrugged. 'Not really. He seemed to be more interested in my dad than anyone.'

'Do you know if he spoke to anyone else about the investigation?

'He might have spoken to Mr Shaw. He lives in our old house. Terry went to look at it, but I don't know what they talked about. I didn't go inside.'

'Did Terry have any opinions about what had happened to your family?' he asked.

'If he did, he didn't tell me. He asked me what I thought. Told me the police are looking at it as a murder enquiry, which means he might not be able to do much. But he said he'd give it a couple of weeks to see if there was anything worth chasing up. He said finding my dad's old address was a start.'

'Have you told anyone what he is doing?'

'Definitely not! He asked me not to mention it to anyone. Said if the press knew he was looking into it, they would be all over us. Pam and Eddie know, of course – my foster parents,' she explained, 'and Mr Shaw might suspect something. I had to ask his permission for Terry to look around the house.'

After a few more questions it was clear there was nothing more the girl could tell him. He asked her for the Shaw's telephone number. Thanked her for her time. 'Any problems give me a call,' he told her. 'Otherwise you won't hear from me again until I have something to tell you.'

They left the McDonalds together. Made for their respective cars. Climbing in he drove from the car park. Received a small nod from the girl as he set off.

Out on Bridport Road he headed into Dorchester. At County Hall he turned towards Hangman's cottage, then headed out of town. A few minutes later he drove into Mayflower Close.

He pulled in, outside number seven. Climbed from the

car and strode up to the front door. He tried the bell, and then the knocker. No one came to the door. Taking out his phone he called the number that Roz had given him He heard a phone ringing inside, but no one picked up.

Ballinger took out a card. Wrote a brief note on the back and pushed it through the letter box. Then he returned to the car, turned it around, and headed back to Sherborne.

Inside the house Frank Shaw watched Ballinger drive away. Picking up the card from behind the door he wrote down the registration number of the Discovery on the front. Then he took out the other card, from the address book, and called the number.

'Hello Mr Dawson,' he said when the call was picked up. 'I just had another visitor.'

15

Tuesday: Week 2

It was ten-o-clock. In Ballymena, newsagent Danny Reid was shutting up his shop. He usually closed at lunch time on Tuesday to go to the cash and carry. But today he had other things to do. He would be back in time for the evening rush.

Leaving the shop, he walked the half mile to his local Presbyterian church. The coming Sunday marked the beginning of heritage week. An annual event during which the interior of the church was set out like a museum. Draped with artefacts, documents, and photographs of bygone days to illustrate the history of the old building, its people, and its place in the community.

Like so many churches in so many towns, the active membership consisted mainly of older members of the community. Tasks like preparing the church for the expected flow of visitors next week had fallen, as usual, to the same dwindling group of stalwarts. Reid was one of them.

Yesterday, the cleaners had moved in. Given the place a bashing, as his mother used to say. Cleaned it from top to bottom. Danny stayed well away from all that. In Reid's world, cleaning was as much a female thing as having children.

Today, other helpers were moving in. Digging out and

assembling display boards and setting up the tables. A few hours today, and few more tomorrow, should see the job done if enough people turned up.

Reid didn't mind giving up his time. He had been baptised and married in this church. It was where he had attended his parents' funeral services and, some years later, that of his brother. It was also the place where his own funeral service would be held one day. But not too soon, he hoped. In truth, the church was as much a part of the fabric of his life as the shop he had been running since the death of his father, who ran it before him.

Stepping into the building he nodded affably to those already there. He joined in with the work. Laying out the display items and chatting as he did so. Soon he found himself emptying out a box of youth club memorabilia. Using Blu-tack, he began sticking pictures of former members and club leaders onto a white board. One of them caught his attention.

'Look at this,' he told retired schoolteacher Annie Bridges. 'Now there's a blast from the past.'

She studied the photograph. 'Should I know him?'

'Probably a little before your time Annie. That's Michael Carroll. Used to live just down the street from us. Funnily enough I had a feller in the shop the other day, asking about him. Michael moved across the water some years back. Now it seems he's gone missing.'

'Poor fellow. Was the man from the police?'

'One of those private detectives, so he said.'

'Will you send him a copy of that?'

'I don't know?' he shrugged, studying the picture. 'It's not going to be much use to him. Michael won't look anything like this now.'

'But if the poor man's gone missing, surely his friends and family might take some comfort from it.'

'I didn't think of that?'

'That's because you're a man, Danny Reid. If my husband went missing, I would want to keep every memory of him I could lay my hands on.'

'You're right!' he told her.

The inside of the church was not well lit, so Danny carried the photograph into the porch and opened the outer door to let in daylight. He attached the black and white image to the noticeboard then took a close-up of it with his mobile phone.

This done, he took the old photograph back into the church and attached it to the history board with the others. Then he sought out the church's unpaid general handyman, retired electrician Graham Rigg. He asked Graham to show him how to send the picture he had taken, to the number Ballinger had left. Minutes later the image was on its way.

16

A light drizzle was falling as Ballinger drove into Lyme Regis. The sat nav took him to Silver Street where he quickly found the access lane leading to the motor-cycle repair shop. A man was standing in the open doorway, smoking an e-cigarette.

Ballinger climbed from the car. The man exhaled a cloud of vapour and watched him approach.

'Alan Badell?'

The man nodded.

'Name's Ballinger. I'm an associate of Terry Dutton. He was here last Thursday.'

'That's right.'

'What did you talk about?'

'Why don't you ask him?'

'I can't. He's lying in Antrim hospital. Someone ran him down with a car.'

Badell looked genuinely surprised. 'Oh, I'm really sorry to hear that. He seemed like an okay bloke. Come inside,' he said, pocketing the e-cig. 'I'll make us a coffee. You can tell me what happened.'

Ballinger was shown into the office. Directed to the same seat Dutton had occupied some days earlier. When the motorbike mechanic went off for the drinks, he studied the workshop layout, He was impressed.

'Nice set-up!' he commented when Badell returned with two mugs. 'I could use some of this kit in my workshop.'

'Are you into bikes?'

'Vintage cars.'

'Rebuilding?'

Ballinger nodded.

'I wouldn't have the patience,' said Badell. 'All that time on one project? It'd do my head in.'

'So, tell me about Dutton,' Ballinger asked.

'He was asking about the Carrolls. I'm ex-job. I was on the Carroll case for a while. He wanted me to tell him what the police knew.'

'And did you?'

'I told him the police knew bugger-all. Still know bugger-all from what I've heard. He said he was looking into the case for the Carroll's daughter.'

'Did he tell you he was going to Ulster?'

'He did! He thought the answer might lie over there. Perhaps he was right. Was it an accident?'

'Not really. He was deliberately run down. Did you tell anyone Dutton was going there?'

A shake of the head. 'Who do I know that would even be interested? People I mix with only talk about bikes.'

'He'd only been in Ulster an hour or so. No one over there knew he was on his way. If someone was waiting for him, and it looks like they were, then someone over here must have tipped them off.'

'Well it wasn't me,' insisted Badell.

The two men chatted further about old cars and motorbikes. When they'd finished drinking their coffees, Ballinger thanked Badell and left him to his work.

Driving out of town he went over the conversation he'd had with the ex-policeman. Badell had appeared open and honest enough. Genuinely taken aback by what had happened to Dutton.

But unless it was pure bad luck – which he did not for one minute believe – the attack on his friend had been orchestrated by someone over here. Since Badell had foreknowledge of the trip, he was currently number one on Ballinger's list of suspects.

Ballinger drove into Dorchester. As he parked the car his phone went.

'Mr Ballinger?' The voice coming through the speaker had a pronounced Ulster accent.

'Speaking!'

'Danny Reid – the newsagent – Ballymena.'

'Yes, hello Mister Reid.'

'I just sent you a picture of an old photograph I found. It's your man, Michael Carroll. It was with some old parish photos we were sorting through. Taken some years back when he was with the youth club table tennis team. We thought there might be someone in his life who would like it. Are you anywhere nearer to finding him?'

'We are not! And to be honest I'm not sure we ever will. But thank you for the photo. His daughter will be pleased. She only has the one photograph of him, taken some years ago, on holiday.'

'Daughter? He has family?'

'Yes. Michael was married to a widow with two children. He adopted them both.'

'Then I hope it gives her some comfort,' offered the newsagent.

'I'm sure it will,' said Ballinger, ending the call.

He opened up his messages. Found the picture. It showed a teenage Michael Carroll smashing down a table tennis ball during the course of some game. He forwarded it on to Roz with the message, *Received from Ballymena. Your Dad in his youth club days.*

Leaving the car he entered the offices of the Dorset Free Herald. It took a standard administration fee of fifteen pounds to give him access to the newspaper's back-issue archives. Hoping to learn something about Michael Carroll, he started at the end of 1999 and worked backwards through every issue, looking for references to the name Carroll.

There were lots of ads for the Carroll tour company within the pages. But it was not until he reached the month of June that he found what he was looking for. A full page spread on the start-up of Dorchester's new business venture, Carroll Tours.

The photograph was typical of its kind. A front-on shot of two new coaches in their impressive livery, parked in a V formation before the company's depot. Standing before the vehicles, flanked by four uniformed drivers, was Michael Carroll.

Because it was a wide angle shot, the people in it looked quite small. Like all newsprint photographs, the picture was made up of ink dots, causing the details to blur out when enlarged. But he was able to see that Carroll had dark hair, and that his lower face was covered by a beard. A pair of sunglasses were perched on his nose. Very shy our Michael Carroll, thought Ballinger.

He moved onto the article. Read it in full. It told him absolutely nothing about Carroll. The founding father of

Carroll Tours was described as 'a local entrepreneur who had recently moved into the area from Northern Ireland.'

Ballinger didn't think the journalist covering the event had received much, if any, background information about the man himself and was having to improvise.

17

Back home in Sherborne, Ballinger was in the barn stripping apart the rear seat of the car he was working on. His phone began to sound. It was Roz.

'Mr Ballinger?'

'Hi Roz. Did you get the photo I sent?'

'I did. That's why I'm calling. I don't know where you found it, but I'm fairly sure this is not my dad.'

'Oh? Why's that?'

'Well to start with, he is holding the bat in his left hand. So he must be left-handed. My dad was not left-handed. He was right-handed.'

'You're sure?' he asked.

'Definitely! He was useless with his left hand. Could barely catch a ball with it. In fact, he was pretty useless at sport, in general. The only game I ever saw him play was chess. He taught me to play – Tony, too, but the game was too slow for my brother.'

'I am sorry about that, Roz. It came from someone who lived near your father when he was young. He must be mistaken. Next time I speak to him I'll check he sent the correct photograph.'

'That's okay. It was a nice gesture.'

'Roz, can I ask you something? Did your father ever talk about his business? How it all started?'

'Not that I can think of. I remember one time when we were talking about the millennium. He said it had given the business a great boost, because of all the visitors it brought to the UK. Generally, though, he didn't talk much about his work. I don't think he was happy there.'

'What made you think that?'

'Because when he sold the business he changed completely. He became a totally different person. A lot happier, and a lot more fun.'

When Roz had rung off, Ballinger checked the picture in his phone. There was no doubt about it! The photograph showed Carroll with the bat in his left hand having just delivered what was, probably, a winning smash. Now why hadn't he noticed that? Dutton would have, he felt sure.

He called Danny Reid. 'Mr Reid it's John Ballinger. I just wanted to let you know I have passed the picture you sent, on to Carroll's daughter.'

'Thank you, Mr Ballinger.'

'I didn't realise Michael was lefthanded?'

'That's what made him such a good player, see? He played against right-handers most of the time, so he became used to it. But most of his opponents struggled against a left-hander. Cack-hand Carroll, they called him. Or the cack-hand kid. He didn't care. He was our secret weapon. Rarely lost a game.'

'Can you remember when he left the province?'

'Ninety-eight, after his mother died. She died late September. I remember that because my brother died in August, the same year. The poor woman had been ill for some time with cancer. I can't say I blame Michael for getting out. There wasn't much for him around here. He'd had a rough time of it, what with the accident and then his mother.

'What accident was that?'

'Oh, it knocked him for six, so it did. He ran into a car with his lorry. Woman driver and her two young sons. All three killed outright. It wasn't his fault. She drove through a red light. He was carrying a full load and had no chance of stopping.

He was never the same after that. He had a breakdown. Gave up his job and packed in driving. At one point he stopped going out altogether. Then, when his mother started with the cancer, he became her full-time carer. When she died, he was off like a shot.'

'Did he sell the family home?'

'Wasn't his to sell. The Carrolls were tenants.'

Ballinger thanked the newsagent and ended the call. He sat there, contemplating what he had just learned.

Nothing added up. Either Dutton had got it wrong and the Michael Carroll who grew up in Ballymena was not the same Michael Carroll that had been father to Roz. Or, if Dutton had got it right, then Roz's father was not who he had claimed to be. He wondered what the chances were that two men called Michael Carroll would leave Ballymena around the same time, in the same year. Not good, he decided.

Still thinking about what he had learned, he called Alex for an update on Terry.

18

Wednesday Week 2

Ballinger was on his second coffee of the day and well into solving the Soduko when his phone went off. It was a mobile phone number he didn't recognise.

'Ballinger.'

'Hello Mr Ballinger, it's Frank Shaw. I'm sorry we missed you the other day.'

'That's okay, Mr Shaw. I am an associate of Terry Dutton. I'm following up on Terry's visit to the house last week, and I wondered if I might call to see you.'

'Well, we're in now if you want to come round.'

Ballenger checked his watch. 'I can do that. I'll be there about lunchtime. Is that alright?'

'That's fine. We'll see you later, then,' and the line went dead.

Just before midday Ballinger pulled in outside the former Carroll house. He went to the front door and tried the bell. No one came. With a feeling of déjà vu, he tried the knocker. Again no one came.

He walked around the house. Through a gate into a well-kept back garden. On the back of the house was a kitchen door. Further along was a sliding patio door that was partially open. Using his sleeve, he pushed the door open wider still. Stuck his head through the gap.

'Hello!' he called out. 'Anyone home?' There was no reply.

Taking care not to touch anything he stepped inside. Found himself in a long, L-shaped, dining room that ran from the back of the house to the front. To his right was an opening that took him through into a kitchen.

Calling out again, he entered the main hallway. Two doors there. One opened into the 'L' of the dining room, the other into a lounge. Both of these rooms were unoccupied.

He walked down the hall towards the front door and stairs. Against the wall stood a telephone table on which reasted an address book. Sticking out from beneath the book's cover was a business card.

Curious, he flipped open the book. There were two cards inside. The one he had pushed through the door on his earlier visit, now with his car's registration number scrawled across it. The other, older and more faded, bore the name Gerald Dawson. Beneath the name was a mobile telephone number.

Taking out his phone he took a photograph of the card. As he did so, he heard the double thud of car doors being pushed shut, outside.

The Shaws were back. Quickly he exited the house the way he had entered. He pushed the patio door shut then loped across the lawn towards the shed. He was peering through the shed window when a uniformed policeman appeared from around the side of the house.

The cop saw him. He said something into his personal radio, then beckoned him over.

'Over here, please!' he ordered. Ballinger strolled nonchalantly towards the cop. 'What are you doing here?'

'I'm looking for Frank Shaw,' answered Ballinger, truthfully. 'I have a meeting with him.'

'In his garden shed?'

'No one came to the door, explained Ballinger patiently. 'I was checking to see if he was out back.'

A second officer arrived. He was shorter than the first. A little overweight.

'How long have you been here?' asked the first cop.

Ballinger shrugged. 'A few minutes. I tried the front door, but no one came. So, I came round the back.'

'Have you been inside the house?' asked the other cop.

'I don't have a key.'

The first officer took out his notebook. 'Name?'

While Ballinger was giving his details, the other policeman began to check out the back of the house. When he tried the patio door it slid open.

'Ted!' he called warningly to his colleague.

The first cop responded immediately. He grabbed hold of Ballinger's arm and spun him round to face the wall. Ballinger made no attempt to resist.

'Hands behind your back!' he was ordered.

Calmly he did as he was told. The handcuffs were expertly slipped over his wrists.

'Wait there!' the cop told his partner. He marched Ballinger from the garden and along the side of the house. 'If there's anyone in there, tell me now,' he commanded.

'I don't know what you're talking about!'

'We had a report of a robbery in progress, here.'

Ballinger shook his head. 'It wasn't me! But if there was someone in there, they'll be long gone by now. Out the front door, while you and your mate were round the back giving me a hard time.'

'Don't come the smart-arse,' warned the officer marching him down the drive. 'That your car?'

Ballenger nodded.

'Where's the keys?'

'Jacket pocket!'

His keys were confiscated. Still handcuffed, he was locked inside the patrol car. He watched the cop return to the house, then he leaned back in the seat and relaxed.

Ten minutes later both police officers returned to the car. The one called Ted climbed into the driving seat. He put in a call for a PNC check on Ballinger's car. When it came back clean, he turned towards the back seat. 'Do you have any identification?'

'Driving license. In my wallet. Inside pocket.'

The driver reached over. He pulled open Ballinger's jacket, slipped his hand into the inside pocket, and pulled out the wallet. From it he removed the driving license and one of the business cards lodged inside. 'That's who I am, and what I do,' Ballinger told him.

The cop checked the photograph on the license. He looked at the business card. 'Security Consultant? What's that about? Burglar alarms?'

'Not home security. Personal security, for VIP's and businessmen. Here and abroad.'

'So, what's your business here?'

'A personal matter.'

'When did you arrange to see Mr Shaw?'

'Couple of hours ago.'

'Well that's where we have a problem, see. The caller told us the Shaws were away this week, and that they had seen someone moving about inside their house?'

Ballinger shrugged. 'Can't help that. Shaw rang me up

this morning and told me to come to the house. He told me they were home, and he that would see me.

I don't know what's going on any more than you do,' he stated, 'but this is the second time I've been here, and the second time there has been no one at home. So why don't you just give me back my things so I can get on with my busy day? You can keep the card, so you'll know where to find me. I'm not going anywhere.'

The two officers exchanged glances. The plump one shrugged. *Your call*, he was saying. The one called Ted thought about it, then slid the license back into the wallet. He climbed from the car and opened the rear passenger door. 'Okay, out you get.'

Ballinger climbed from the car. The policemen removed the cuffs.

'Keep yourself available Mr Ballinger,' he was told as his possessions were returned. 'Perhaps they just forgot to lock the door. But if this turns out to be something else, you'll be hearing from us again.'

Ballinger nodded. He walked back to his car and climbed in. Firing up the ignition he did a faultless three-point turn and drove away.

19

On the way back to Sherborne he tried to make sense of what had just happened. Had he been lured to the house? The inviting door left open to entice him inside. It certainly seemed that way. If so, the trap had almost worked. Had he not heard the police car arrive, they would have caught him in there. He would now be attempting to talk himself out of a burglary charge.

He had been set up, he felt sure. It seemed that, like Dutton before him, he had attracted someone's attention. Someone who does not want anyone snooping around the Carroll case. The fact that they knew exactly where he was when they called the cops, told him he was either being followed or tracked.

Arriving home he drove into the barn. From his samples case he took out his bug wand and checked the car. It didn't take long. The tracker was a clip-on, attached to the radiator grill. Quite small, and powered by a watch battery, the device would only work for a few days.

It would not take long for someone to fit a device like this, he decided. Just a second or two. Yesterday he had called at Badell's place. He had also left his car close to the newspaper offices in Dorchester.

It was just possible, he supposed, that someone had attached the tracker whilst his car stood on a busy street in the town centre. But his money was on Badell.

It would have been so easy for the ex-policeman to clip it into place when he went to make the coffee. He wondered if there was a similar device on Dutton's car.

Ballinger removed the tracker and binned it. He was about to leave the barn when his phone went. It was Alex.

'I'm at the hospital. The doctors are quite pleased with Terry's progress. They say if nothing changes, he should be coming home next week.'

'That's great,' he told her. 'I'm really pleased. Listen Alex, I'm coming over there tomorrow. Things are happening here, and I need to talk to Terry. He needs to be put in the picture.'

'In that case you can have him all to yourself,' she told him. 'It will give me a break. A chance to do some shopping and take a look around Belfast.'

'You sure?'

'I'm sure. But come back to the hotel for dinner, will you. My tab this time.'

'You're on!'

He went into the house and opened up his laptop. Brought up flights to Belfast. Tomorrow morning's flight was already fully booked. He checked today's flights. The next one was at six-thirty. The last flight of the day. There were three seats left. He booked one of them.

As there was still the possibility that he was being followed he decided not to advertise his movements. He called a taxi company he often used.

'It's John Ballinger. I need a ride to Exeter airport.'

'From your address?' he was asked.

'No! Tell him to pick me up outside the White Hart in half an hour.'

He packed an overnight bag then pulled on a pair of overshoes. Exiting via the back door, he climbed into the field that ran behind his property. Walked diagonally across the pasture and made for a distant gap in the hedge. Climbing the stile that guarded the opening, he dropped into the rear car park of White Hart.

The taxi was waiting for him by the roadside. He removed the overshoes. Left them against the back wall of the building and climbed into the vehicle. He had no doubt the shoes would still be there when he returned.

20

Thursday. Week 2

The next morning, Ballinger left the Premier Inn in Belfast's Titanic quarter. Heading north he called into a greasy spoon on the edge of the city. The place did the best Irish Breakfast in the Province.

When he had eaten, he took out his phone. Keyed in a number he hadn't called for some time, hoping it would still be in use. He smiled when he recognised the bass tones of the man who answered.

'Beagle calling Peel,' he intoned.

There was a momentary pause. Then the loud, deep, voice boomed into his ear. 'Ballinger, you murderous bugger. How are you?'

'I'm good, Col. You?'

'I'm still here so I must be doing something right. What can I do for you Sandy?'

'What makes you think I want something?'

'Listen, I get calls from the police. I get calls from lawyers. Calls from TV people. I even receive calls from historians. Can you imagine that? We're history already. Almost every call I get is from someone wanting the inside story on some case I was involved with. Sometimes, even, cases I wasn't involved with. What I hardly ever get are calls from old friends, asking how I am. Telling me they are on the way up here to share a bottle.'

'Funny you should say that,' grinned Ballinger. 'I was wondering if later on today would be a good time to pop in for a drink, and a chat about old times? And, whilst we're at it, I'd like to pick your brains on a small matter I'm working on.'

'Any time is a good time, Sandy. I don't go far these days. Where are you?'

'Antrim. Are you still in your place by the lake?'

'I am. But what the hell are you doing, in Antrim? I thought you'd had a bellyful of that place.'

'Long story. I'll tell you when I see you.' He ended the call.

Paying for his meal he left the café then drove to the Dunsilly.

'Change of plan,' he told a surprised Alex when she opened the door of her room. 'Couldn't get a morning flight so I came over last night. You still going sightseeing?'

'Yes, and shopping.'

'Want me to run you into Belfast?'

'No that's okay. I've booked a taxi to take me on a sight-seeing tour. He'll be here in half an hour.'

'Be sure to take in the Titanic Experience,' he advised her. 'It's well worth a visit.'

'Thank you, I will.'

'There's another change of plan,' he told her, apologetically. 'I'll have to cancel our dinner I'm afraid. When I've seen Terry I'm going back to the mainland. There's a man I need to see who might have some answers for us.'

'Don't worry, I'll be fine. I'll have my lunch out, instead. Any good eating places you can recommend?'

He gave her the names of three good luncheon restaurants in the city. 'I can recommend the Italian, especially,' he said. 'But they're all great. At least, they were, the last time I was over here.'

They went down to the lobby together and waited for Alex's taxi to arrive. Once she had left for the city he went into the bar. He ordered a coffee. Picked up a newspaper then sat drinking coffee. Killing time.

21

Dutton was surprised when Ballinger entered the room. But he was happy enough to see him. 'Don't get me wrong. I love Alex to bits, but it's so good to see another face in here. I'm bored out of my skull.' He studied Ballinger shrewdly. 'So, how is the investigation going?'

Ballinger was surprised. 'Alex told you?'

Dutton grinned. 'No. You just did.' He pulled himself up into a sitting position. 'I noticed how Alex became evasive whenever I mentioned Roz, or the Carrolls. So, I figured you must be up to something.'

'Smart-arse copper,' growled Ballinger.

'Ex-copper! So come on, give! I might not be able to run around, but I can still think.'

Ballinger sat down on a visitor's chair. 'To be honest, I didn't mean to get involved in the Carroll thing at all. I was just looking to find out why someone took the trouble to knock the legs from under you? And if it's any comfort, I don't think they intended to kill you. I think it was just a warning. A chance for you to walk away from the Carroll case. Trouble is, once I got started, I found myself being pulled in deeper.'

He opened up the photograph on his phone. Held it out for Dutton to see.

'Do I know him?' asked the detective.

'Michael Carroll. In the flower of his youth.'

'Really? Where'd you get that?'

'Danny Reid. Ballymena's friendly, neighbourhood, newsagent. The one you almost got to meet. Seems that young Carroll was the star of the local youth club's table-tennis team. All the more formidable a player, by virtue of being left-handed.'

Dutton looked closer at the image. 'I can see that.'

'I knew you would. The problem is, according to Roz Carroll not only was her father right-handed, he was also totally inept at any kind of sport.'

'Really?'

'Really!'

'Oh shit!' breathed Dutton.

'So, either one of them has got it wrong, which I feel is extremely unlikely? Or the Dorset businessman calling himself Michael Carroll, late of Ballymena, was not Michael Carroll at all.'

'You don't suppose there could be two Michael Carrolls?'

'I'm sure there are. But not, I think, both leaving Ballymena at the same time. But let me put together what I have learned.

According to Reid, Carroll left Ulster late nineteen ninety-eight. An unemployed lorry driver looking to start a new life on the mainland. Eight months later, according to the local paper, he turns up in Dorchester and starts up his own coach touring company.

How did he do that? This is a man who hadn't worked for months. Stuck at home, caring for his sick mother. So where did he get his start-up money?'

'The bank?'

'Not without security. Which he didn't have. And I checked the Company history. Carroll Tours started life with two brand-new, luxury, coaches.

They would have cost what, back then? A hundred grand each? Plus, garaging. Office space. Fuel. Drivers' salaries - and that's two drivers per coach if you are going nationwide, which he was. Then there was office staff, and at least one mechanic?'

'So, he was bankrolled?'

'Quite possibly. But who is going to invest that kind of money in a penniless lorry driver on the wrong side of a nervous breakdown?'

Dutton nodded. 'So you're saying that somewhere between leaving Ballymena and arriving in Dorchester, the real Michael Carroll disappears – '

' – and Roz's father assumes his identity,' finished Ballinger.

'Why would someone do that?'

'Ulster, Terry. Back then the place had lots of people with good reasons to do a vanishing act. And not just those wanted by the police.'

Dutton shook his head. 'This is turning into a real can of worms, isn't it?'

'It is. I am not surprised someone is out to stop us.

'Us?'

'Someone tried to have me arrested for burglary. They lured me to the Shaw house. Left the door open for me to walk in. Then called the police.'

'What happened?'

'Luckily I heard them coming. Got out of there fast. I thought it was the Shaws, but it was the police.'

'But who would connect you with me?'

'My money is on Alan Badell. You called to see him, mentioned you were heading over here, and look what happened to you. I called on him, and someone put a tracker on my car so they could set me up. I think Badel did that. Did he go off and make you a coffee when you called?'

'Yes, he did.'

'Then he probably stuck one on your car, too. As soon as you headed out to the airport, they would have known you were on your way here.'

'Who's doing this?' asked Dutton.

'Wrong question, Terry! Ask yourself this, who do we know who would go to great lengths, short of killing people, to protect both themselves and their dirty little secrets?'

Dutton Blinked. 'Are you saying the Intelligence Services are behind this?'

'Well, who didn't want the police digging into Carroll's Irish background when he disappeared? Who was lurking behind glass doors to make sure this did not happen?'

'Shit!' swore Dutton, again.

'How right you are. Because if my take on this is correct, we are both well and truly up to our necks in the stuff. Not just for interfering in an ongoing police operation, which is bad enough, but possibly for threatening to uncover some security operation that has lain buried, since the troubles ended.' He paused to let this sink in. Then went on.

'Perhaps on this occasion we should do the smart thing, Terry. Take the hint and walk away? For I can't help feeling that if we don't do that, then things might start getting pretty complicated for us, very quickly?'

Dutton nodded, but without conviction. 'And what about Roz?' he asked. 'If the Security Services have information relating to the disappearance of her family, do you not think she has a right to know?'

Ballinger shrugged. 'I hear what you're saying. But on the other hand, do you really want to be the one to tell her that her father was not who he claimed to be. That he might even be a killer?'

'A killer?'

'Think about it? If he was not Michael Carroll, what did he do with the real one?'

Dutton shook his head in frustration. But his expression remained grim, his eyes angry. Ballinger sighed. 'You're not going to drop this, are you? This is not about Roz, now, is it? It's about that nosey copper inside of you, wanting to know what's going on?'

'Partly. But it's also about wanting to know who put me in this place. Alright, there's no lasting damage done, but there might have been? They might have killed me. Or put me in a wheelchair, for life. No, I'm sorry mate. They're not getting away with that, whoever they are.'

He looked at Ballinger. 'If you want to bail out, Sandy, that's fine. I'll handle it from here. At the end of the day this is my case – my risk.'

'Cobblers,' voiced Ballinger. 'You won't last two minutes without me watching your back, and you know it! Look at you! You can't even walk.'

'Yes I can. I walked to the loo this morning. Twice.'

'Oh, well that's good! So, the next time they come after you, you can throw loo rolls at them. That'll make them think twice, won't it? And what are you going to tell Roz?' he asked.

'Until we know for sure what this is about, I'm telling her nothing. I promised her two weeks, and that's what she is going to get, once I get out of here. Only then will I decide what to tell her, and how far to push this.'

'Two weeks? Okay! I'll go with that.'

'Thank you. So, what's our next move?'

'Your next move is to stay where you are and get well. I'm taking a trip to the Lake District to visit an old friend. Did I ever tell you I was in Ulster during the troubles?'

'No.'

'Well I was. This guy is someone I used to work for. Ex Special Branch. He knows everything there is to know about what was going on over here, back in the day.'

'That's good. But you will keep me informed, won't you?'

'Any developments you'll be the first to know, after me.' Ballinger rose to leave. 'Good to see you on the mend, Terry.'

'Thanks!' said Dutton. 'And stay out of trouble!'

'No chance!'

22

It cost just nineteen pounds and ninety-nine pence for a Ryanair flight from Belfast to Manchester. At Manchester airport Ballinger hired a car and joined the M60 ring road. He took the M61 towards Preston, then swung onto the M6 northbound and stayed with it.

At junction 40 he left the motorway and took the A66 heading West. He skirted around Keswick and stayed on the same road as it swung north, following the shoreline of Bassenthwaite lake.

Two hours after leaving the airport, he passed Thornthwaite village. Here he turned right towards the lake, following a driveway that brought him to a former coaching inn nestled against the shore. Pulling onto a flagged parking area he stopped the car.

Ballinger climbed out. He locked up the car and approached the door. It was open.

'Come in, Sandy!' called a voice from within.

He pushed through into a low, but spacious, lounge. Rising from a comfy-looking armchair next to a stone fireplace, was a stocky individual in his mid-sixties. The man's strong features were decorated by a neatly trimmed grey beard. His head was topped with short grey hair.

'Hello Col,' nodded Ballinger, warmly shaking the man's outstretched hand.

'Grab a seat,' the man pointed to a chair on the other side of the fireplace. A small coffee table sat between the two. On it stood a bottle of Bushmills sixteen-year-old single malt whiskey, and two glasses. Each glass held a good measure of the golden liquid.

Ballinger sat down. Studied the man opposite. Colin Mackay had not changed significantly since the two men had last met. The wiry frame and the strong grip were still there. The dark eyes that regarded him still held the steely gaze of the man who had given Ballinger's SAS troop their operational intelligence until their tour of duty ended, back in 1995.

With two ruined marriages behind him, McKay had sacrificed much to his single-minded pursuit of those who chose to make war in his beloved Ulster. His dedication and successes were recognised both in Belfast and London, taking him to the very top of the command chain.

But the Good Friday agreement had swept away much of the old order, and McKay with it. Pushed into early retirement he took the pension, left the province, and moved to this Cumbrian backwater. Far enough away from those he had once thought were his friends, and others he knew would always be his enemies.

Calling himself a full-time alcoholic, and part-time artist, he now spent his days drinking his favourite Irish tipple and painting passable landscapes that he sold on to the world's tourists, via several Lakeland shops.

'Peel and Beagle,' grinned Ballinger. 'So, who came up with those call signs, anyway.'

'Not guilty!' Mackay lifted his hands and shoulders in in a Gallic shrug. 'But appropriate, do you not think? The classic hunter and his hounds.' He picked up his glass and raised it in a salute. 'Happy days!'

'Not so sure about happy,' Ballinger lifted his own glass. 'Certainly interesting.'

Mackay threw back the drink. Ballinger sipped at his.

'So, what can I do for you, Sandy?'

'Well, to start with, you can tell me about Gerald Dawson.'

'Gerry Dawson? Now there's a prime example of how low humanity can sink. D'you know he was collecting a cash bounty from the loyalists, for every poor bugger he set up for them. Some of his victims were not even active republicans. But if their name came to his attention, they were targeted anyway. What a bastard he was! Did you ever meet him?'

Ballinger shook his head. 'No. But I might be about to. His name keeps coming up in an investigation I am involved with.'

'Then watch your back. He is a nasty piece of work.'

'Thanks. I'll bear that in mind. Okay,' he began, 'I'll tell you a story. An Ulster man turns up in Dorset in late ninety-eight. Calls himself Michael Carroll, from the town of Ballymena. As soon as he arrives there, he starts splashing out big money on a new business venture.

Twenty years down the line an investigation into his background reveals that before leaving Ulster, Michael Carroll was just an out of work truck driver. That he set off for the mainland, looking to make a new start, with nothing but a few quid and a ferry ticket in his pocket.

There is a now a strong suspicion that the man in Dorset claiming to be Michael Carroll, was not him at all. Which raises the question, who the hell was he?

So, in essence, I am looking for someone who left Ulster in late '98. Someone with both the acumen and the funding to set himself up in business, finance a wealthy lifestyle to go with it, and then make a small fortune. All whilst using the identity of a small-time, penniless, lorry driver from Ballymena.'

'Carroll?' said McKay, thoughtfully. 'Isn't he the fella who disappeared with his family, what, five – six years back? I remember all the hoo-ha about them. Why are you interested in him?'

'I'm helping a friend. He is currently in hospital, in Antrim. Put there by someone who didn't like him asking questions in Carroll's old back yard.'

'I see,' nodded Mckay. 'This recent information you mention. Are the police looking at it?'

'No. It was there to be found when the Carrolls went missing. But the Dorset police decided not to look. Their investigation was – *refocussed* – is the word I would use, by the Northern Ireland desk in London.'

'Dawson?'

'The same.'

Mackay nodded thoughtfully. He re-filled his glass and offered the bottle, which Ballinger waved away. 'You're in my fiefdom,' he reminded his guest, putting down the bottle. 'Drinking is almost obligatory.'

He poured the liquid down his throat then looked at Ballinger. 'Late ninety-eight, you say! Well, the first name that comes to mind is Joe Maguire. But he can't be your man.'

'Why not?'

'He's dead.'

'Okay! Who was he, then?'

'Joseph McGuire was an accountant. A fixer and friend to tax-dodgers, criminals, and anyone else who needed a financial wizard who was as bent as they were. At the back end of ninety-eight McGuire did a runner.

It was big news in Ulster. Turns out he had been syphoning off clients' money for years, then playing sleight of hand to cover his tracks.

Before he did his moonlight, he looted as many accounts as he could, and put most of the money offshore. About three million, they reckoned, and that was a conservative estimate, based just on the money that was reported stolen. There were others who were not in any position to complain. Amongst them, I dare say, some very angry paramilitaries. It is thought that the total figure he filched was closer to five million.

Rumour had it that he'd gone to Australia, or South America. But he might have put that about himself. Lots of people did their best to track him down, including us, but he was never found.

Then, a few years later, he turned up. Or what was left of him turned up. Someone, obviously, had caught up with him. He had been kneecapped, then shot in the head. The classic paramilitary execution. Turns out he'd only made it as far as the mainland.'

'Where was he found?'

'Scotland. The money was never recovered. It still sits in his offshore bank accounts waiting for him to spend it. Look him up if you like. But he can't be your man. He was positively identified through his DNA.'

'Can you think of anyone else?'

'Not off the top of my head. There was a lot of movement after peace was established, but that was more into the noughties. A bit outside your time scale.'

'Did McGuire have a partner?'

'I know where you're going. Did someone help him get away, and then kill him and take off with the money. That would be ironic, wouldn't it? And it is a possibility, I suppose. But, generally, McGuire worked alone. And with good reason. He was ripping off too many of the wrong kind of people to risk sharing what he was doing, with anyone. Even his brother, who was his business partner, didn't have a clue what he was up to.'

McKay refilled his glass. 'Could be your mystery man was bankrolled by the paramilitaries. They had the money to invest. Especially with everything winding down. Tell you what, give me a day or two to make some enquiries. See if any other names crop up.' He pointed at Ballinger's glass. 'Meanwhile, stop being so anti-social and finish that off so I can refill your glass.'

'I am driving, you know.'

'No you're not. You'll never make it back to Manchester for the last flight. Best you stay here tonight, then get off to an early start in the morning. That way we can spend the evening reminiscing about the old days and knocking back a glass or two. What d'you think?'

23

Friday. Week 2

Ballinger awoke in a strange bed. He had a raging headache and an upset stomach. Shaved and showered, he washed down a couple of paracetamols with a glass of unpasteurised milk from Mackay's fridge then answered his ringing phone. It was Alex.

'You alright?' she asked. 'You sound different?'

'Sorry,' he told her. 'Bit of a bender last night.'

'Where are you?'

'North Lakes. I was chasing a lead and got held up. I'll be heading home, soon. How was your day?'

'Okay, I suppose.' She sounded a little bit down. 'Perhaps I should have waited until Terry could be with me. It wasn't much fun on my own.'

'Well, Belfast isn't going anywhere. You'll be able to show him the sights when he's fit.'

'I think the hospital will discharge him, soon. There's not a lot more they can do for him. He just needs rest to let his body heal. They've been really good here, but we'll be glad to get back to Dorset.'

'I can understand that. I'm just sorry you had to get caught up in all this.'

'It's not your fault. It was Terry who started the digging. Me who helped push him into it.'

'And me who might have made it worse.'

'Terry told me last night that you don't think Roz's father was the real Michael Carroll. Is that true?'

'It's looking that way. I'm not sure how anyone is going to break that piece of news to the girl? As if she hasn't had enough upset in her life, she may now be about to discover that her old man was an imposter. Possibly, even, a murderer.'

'Perhaps it would be better if she wasn't told.'

'I'm with you on that Alex. Try selling it to Terry for me, will you.'

After taking leave of his host and promising to call again, Ballinger headed south for Keswick. Taking a more leisurely route, he drove down through the towns and villages of the Lake District.

He was glad he did. The unhurried pace, and the scenery, enabled him to shake off the hungover feeling he was carrying. Somewhere above Lancaster he joined the M6, heading south. By the time he reached Manchester airport he was ready for some lunch.

He sat down to a light snack, then booked onto the afternoon city hopper to Exeter. Before boarding he called his local taxi service and arranged for a pick-up. By five-thirty he was back in Sherborne, climbing into his overshoes outside the White Hart.

Back at home, he made himself a coffee. Took it up to his study. Sitting at the desk his fingers automatically brushed along the edge of the bottom drawer. He looked down. This particular drawer was always left open a fraction, so he would know if anyone had been through his desk. Now it was pushed right home.

Carefully he checked the rest of the study. There did

not appear to be anything missing. He opened his samples case and took out the bug wand. Then he systematically went through the house, looking out for anything missing or anything that should not be there.

Once he had cleared the house he moved into the barn. Twenty minutes later he made a discovery.

At the end of the workbench stood an ancient, oak, dresser. It was used for storing nuts, bolts, washers, and other small components. After checking the drawers and cavities, he carefully inched the dresser forward. Shone his torch into the gap behind. There, standing on end between the back of the dresser and the wall, was a chocolate box.

Removing the box, he placed it on the work bench. It was taped shut so he cut the tape, took off the lid, and stared at the contents. Four ladies' diamond rings: two gent's gold rings: a diamond pendant on a gold chain: and two gold watches, one lady's and one gent's. The man's watch bore an inscription. *Presented to Frank Shaw on his retirement. June 2016.*

He put the lid back on the box and continued searching until he was sure the barn was bug-free, and nothing else had been hidden.

Returning to the house he placed the box on the kitchen table. He went up to his study and fast-played through his security video footage. All four cameras had lost nearly two hours of video from between three and five-o-clock that morning.

This looked like a further attempt to have him arrested for breaking into the Shaw house. This time with physical evidence planted, for the police to find. Whoever was doing this was extremely clever, and professional.

He had thought his home burglar-proof. With all the latest security technology, he should have been alerted the moment anyone came near his property. But he had received no alert. The whole system, along with the cameras, had been temporarily disabled.

There were very few specialists who could by-pass a system like the one he had installed. Only someone with expertise of the very highest level.

Something else struck him. In spite of going to extraordinary lengths to ensure no one saw him set off on his journey to Ulster, someone knew he was going to be away from his property last night.

His decision visit McKay had been spontaneous. Taken when he awoke, on Thursday morning, in the Belfast Premier Inn. He had told no one he was going, except Terry and Alex. And he had not told them he would be staying overnight, simply because he had not been planning to.

So either he was under surveillance, or someone who knew his movements last night had been talking to the wrong people. He hoped it was the former.

These attempts to divert him from the case told him nothing about who was behind all this. But they did confirm that looking at the Carrolls' disappearance had been the trigger for all that was happening. Dutton had been attacked the moment he set foot in Ulster. Now he himself was being targeted, in a more creative way, for taking up where Dutton had been forced to leave off.

But by who? Certainly not the police? They would react far more directly if someone rocked their boat.

His money was still on the security services. They had the resources, they were largely accountable to no-one but themselves. Warning someone off by knocking them over with a car was just the kind of thing they might do. Especially if that someone was about to shine a light onto their dirty laundry, and Ulster's recent history held an abundance of dirty laundry from all sides.

He took out his phone. Checked the number he had captured from the card that was tucked in the phone book, inside the Shaw house. He punched it in.

The number rang for a while. No one picked up. He was just about to close the call when someone answered.

'Who is this?' asked the voice.

'Good evening Mr Dawson,' said Ballinger brightly. 'It's John Ballinger. I think it's time you and I had a little chat, don't you?'

The phone was shut off immediately. Ballinger tried calling back but found the number unobtainable. He suspected it would stay that way. But at least the man was now aware that his card had been marked.

When darkness fell, he re-packed, and sealed, the box of valuables in a plastic bag. Donning overshoes, he collected a spade and climbed into the field behind the house. Followed the hedge to one corner of the pasture.

He dug a hole in the ground, behind a drinking trough. Dropped in the bag, then filled in the hole and stamped down the earth. At some point in the future he would need to find a way to return the stolen goods. Or permanently lose them. But for now, he simply wanted them away from the house and its immediate surround.

The next morning he was in the barn, bright and early. With little he could do until McKay got back to him, he spent the morning working. He broke off for a liquid lunch at the pub and was back at work when the phone rang, just after four pm. It was Alex.

'We're coming home,' she announced. 'Tomorrow morning. I've organised an air ambulance to pick us up at Aldergrove and fly us back to Bristol. Terry's car is still at the airport there, so I'll drive him home. I hate to ask, Sandy, but would you mind meeting us there. Terry will be in a wheelchair. I might struggle, getting him into the car.'

'No problem, what time is your flight?'

'Eleven-o-clock. We should be in arrivals for twelve-thirty. That okay?

'That's fine Alex, I'll be there.'

'Thanks again Sandy, you're a star.'

Ballinger took off his work clothes. Then he went for a shower before settling down for the evening.

24

Sunday. Week 3

Frank Shaw sat on the damp, concrete, floor. His back was against a steel roof support, his hands tied together behind it. He was hungry. Worst still, he was unbelievably thirsty. He tried to think how long they had been there. How long since he'd had anything to drink. Two days? Three? He couldn't think. He had lost all sense of time.

Turning his head, he looked at his wife. She was attached to a similar pillar on the other side of the aisle. Her head was down, chin resting on the top of her chest. She hadn't moved for hours.

'Helen,' he tried to speak, through the tape over his mouth. Catching the muffled sound, she lifted her head. Looked at him with hopeless eyes then turned away.

Angrily he struggled against the bonds. Tried again to pull his hands free. As always, it was useless. His struggles simply caused more damage to his wrists. He slumped back down and stared ahead.

Never had he felt so uncomfortable. His trousers were wet, he smelled disgusting. His buttocks burned with infection from sitting in his own dirt and urine.

He had no idea where they were. Nor how they had got here. He recalled going into the garage to bring out the car. After that he remembered nothing, until he came to in this place.

A long sigh escaped his lips. He closed his eyes. Switched off to his surroundings. Allowed his mind to drift. Not for the first time he found himself thinking about Terry Waite. As a hostage, Waite had endured five long years chained to a radiator. Five years? How does anyone survive that? But at least Waite was given food and water to keep him alive. Not left to die slowly, of dehydration and starvation.

Time passed. Shaw sank into a stupor. Minutes, or hours, later he was awakened by a sound. Helen had heard it too. She looked at him with an expression that lay somewhere between hope and fear.

Footsteps came down the walkway behind them. A man stepped into view. He turned and regarded the captives, dispassionately. Shaw did not recognise him.

The stranger put a hand into his pocket. He pulled out a small black bundle, and some string. A piece of the bundle dropped to the floor. The man tugged at what remained in his hand, opening it up. It was a bin liner. He stepped towards Shaw.

Shaw's stomach went hollow with fear. No, he thought, this could not be happening. Desperately he looked into the man's expressionless eyes as the open bag was thrust towards his head.

'Why?' he tried to ask through the gag.

The man ignored him. He tied the bag securely over his head then, picking up the one he had dropped, he moved towards the woman.

25

Ballinger waited in the arrivals hall. He had set off in good time for Bristol airport, but the Sunday traffic had been remarkably light. He had arrived at the airport with lots of time to spare before the Dutton's flight was due.

Fifty minutes later, Terry and Alex came through into arrivals. Alex led the way. An attendant from the air ambulance walked behind, pushing Dutton along in a wheelchair. After greeting his friends, Ballinger led the way to the pick-up point.

'Where's your car?' he asked.

'The long stay car park!'

'Give me the keys. I'll go and bring it.'

Armed with the keys Ballinger walked to the car park. It took a few minutes to locate Dutton's car. He checked it over. Clipped to the rear wiper blade was a small tracker, identical to the one he found on his own car. He took it off. Left it on top of the pay station.

Back at the pick-up point, helped by the ambulance attendant, Dutton was smoothly manoeuvred into the front passenger seat.

'Sorry Sandy,' apologised Alex, 'I didn't know we'd have help, or I wouldn't have had you trailing up here.'

'I would have come anyway,' he assured her. 'Just wait here until I get my car, and I'll escort you home.'

Minutes later the two-car convoy left the airport and headed for the M5. They stopped only once on the seventy-mile journey south. Arrived at the Duttons' cottage, in Portland, just after three-o-clock. Ballinger helped Dutton from the car, and into the house.

They made themselves at home. Re-heated, and then dined upon, the Indian takeaway they had picked up in Weymouth. Then, while Alex phoned around telling her friends that she and Terry were back home, Ballinger told Dutton about the intrusion into his property, and the unexpected gifts left there.

'They are determined to get you out of the way, aren't they?'

'Then they're going to be disappointed. The thing that bothers me is how they knew I'd be away from home.'

'Who knew, apart from yourself?'

'Colin McKay.'

'That's a pretty short list,' observed Dutton.

'Isn't it just.'

At five-thirty Ballinger set off for home. Driving past Dorchester he thought about Roz, and the Pandora's box she had opened.

He hoped she would be able to walk away from this without too much grief, although this now seemed unlikely. Already enough doubts had come to light about the girl's father, to suggest that there was little likelihood of her getting the kind of closure she was so desperately seeking.

26

Monday. Week 3

Detective Sergeant Karen Walsh pulled the car into the kerb. Beside her, DI Paul Lockwood wound down the window and flashed his warrant card at the uniform. The constable swung open the rusty gates. Walsh drove through, into a large, weed-festooned, cobbled yard.

Apart from a few items of rubbish thrown over the high walls by fly tippers, the yard was empty. To their left stood the derelict building, its dirty windows mainly intact.

Next to a shuttered loading gate stood a wooden door that still bore traces of industrial green paint. It, too, was guarded by a uniformed constable. Lockwood thought he looked about fifteen.

'Is it me?' asked Lockwood. 'Or are bobbies getting younger?'

'It's you!' Walsh told him. 'You're beginning to sound like my old grandad.' They climbed from the car and opened the boot. 'What is this place?' she asked.

'Old engineering works. Been empty for years. Made munitions during the first world war. Torpedoes for submarines, during the second.'

'Why is it still standing?'

'Belongs to a German investment company, or so I heard. Ironic that, don't you think? I'm sure they'll redevelop the site when times get better.'

They pulled on their white coveralls and gloves, then shut the tailgate. They approached the door. 'First responder?' Lockwood asked the uniform.

The PC nodded.

'Your first murder?'

'Yes, sir.'

'Hope you weren't sick in there.'

'No sir.' The young constable opened the door. Held it for them while they slipped into their overshoes. 'Straight ahead,' he told them, as they stepped into the building. 'Then through the next set of doors. They're halfway down the next walkway.'

The door closed noisily behind them. They were in a large empty room. Dimly lit, by light seeping in through dirty windows. A concrete aisle stretched ahead of them between rows of rusty iron pillars supporting the ceiling. They walked down to a pair of rubber swing doors and pushed their way through.

The room they entered was much like the first, only smaller. Ten yards ahead were the bodies. One on each side of the walkway. The man and the woman sat on the floor, their backs to the pillars. Each had their wrists secured behind with cable ties. Their upper torsos were slumped forward. Both victims had black, plastic, bags over their heads, tied at the throat with what looked like green garden string.

Walsh took the woman. The smell of urine and faeces from both bodies was strong. 'Bit ripe!' she commented. 'Been here a day or two.' She unzipped the top of the coverall. Reached into her shirt pocket and pulled out a pack of strong mints. 'Want a mint?' she asked, popping one into her mouth.

'I'm okay,' he told her. He had confronted worse-smelling corpses than these in his time. Squatting down, he tugged open the man's jacket. Reached a gloved hand into the inside pocket and removed the victim's wallet. From outside the building, came the distant wailing of approaching sirens.

'Here comes the cavalry,' voiced Walsh

Lockwood nodded absently. He opened the wallet and pulled out a driving license. 'Frank Shaw,' he read out, aloud. 'Seven, Mayflower Close, Dorchester.' The words printed on the small plastic card struck a chord. 'Mayflower Close? Oh shit!' he exclaimed, turning to his companion. 'You know who lived at number seven, Mayflower Close, don't you?

'Who?'

'Only the bloody Carroll family! That's who!'

'Jesus!' breathed Walsh. 'What do we do?'

'We call the boss, that's what we do.' Stepping away from the bodies he unzipped the top of his coveralls and reached inside for his phone. 'Better grab hold of your tin hat, Kas!' he told her. 'This is going to go bloody nuclear!'

27

They arrived at four-o-clock in the afternoon. Ballinger was in the kitchen. Standing at the sink. Cleaning a carburettor head with a tooth brush. He heard the vehicles screech to a halt. Car doors opening and closing. Then a loud hammering on the front door.

'Police! Open the door!'

He went to open it before they decided to break it down. A group of police officers in assault uniforms were outside. One of them was carrying a ram.

A plain-clothed officer pushed his way to the front.

'John Ballinger?' The man held up a warrant card and sheet of paper. 'DCI Penny! We have a warrant to search these properties. Stand aside please.'

Ballinger said nothing. Leaving the door open he returned to the kitchen. Dried his hands and sat at the table. Penny, and a young female constable, followed him through. The rest fanned out into the house.

'Coffee?' he asked.

'No thank you!' said the detective.

Through the window Ballinger saw the cop with the ram, and a group of uniforms, making for the barn. 'Barn door's locked,' he said. He pointed to a row of keys hanging on the wall. 'End key on the left, if you don't mind, before your storm troopers smash it down.'

The DCI nodded to the constable who collected the key and hurried out the side door. Penny looked down at him. 'You don't seem over surprised to see us?'

Ballinger smiled. 'I was tipped off. I have a source in Divisional HQ.'

'Very funny, Ballinger.'

Ballinger raised his eyes to the policeman. 'What makes you think I'm joking?'

Ignoring the remark, the detective opened the door into the lounge. 'Don't go anywhere,' he ordered, stepping into the room. 'I'll be wanting a chat later.'

'I'll want more than a chat if you cause any damage!'

The WPC re-joined Ballinger in the kitchen. Stayed with him to make sure he didn't attempt to hide, or move, anything.

The search was intense. It took over two hours. At one point a uniformed sergeant entered the kitchen to search the place.

'What's in here?' he asked, indicating a padlocked corner cupboard.

'Shotgun.'

'Licensed?'

Ballinger nodded.

'Open it please.'

Ballinger took the keys from his pocket and opened up the gun cupboard. The sergeant lifted out the gun. He broke it open. Checked the empty breech. After closing the break, he hefted it to his shoulder and sighted along the barrels.

'Nice gun,' he remarked, returning it to the rack. 'Do much shooting?'

'Only at people who piss me off,' said Ballinger, drily.

'I'll take that as a joke,' grunted the policeman, peering inside the cartridge box. Satisfied, he finally closed the door and snapped the lock shut. His eyes strayed to the sink. He peered at the engine part. 'That old car you have in the barn, what is it?'

'It's a Brough.'

'I thought Brough made motorbikes.'

'He did! He made some cars too. That's a drop head convertible. Nineteen-thirty-five. Are you interested in vintage cars?'

The man shook his head. 'Not on my pay. But I do have a Norton Commando motorbike I inherited, from the old man.'

'Commando? That's nineteen-sixties, right?'

'Sixty-eight he bought it.'

'You ride it?'

The man nodded. 'I keep it ticking over.'

Finishing his search, the sergeant left Ballinger alone. Time passed. He heard feet stomping about upstairs, Furniture being moved. He hoped they didn't leave too much of a mess, but he wasn't hopeful.

At last the search was over. The uniforms returned to their vans. The door opened and DCI Penny walked in. With him was the sergeant.

'Find anything interesting?' asked Ballinger.

Penny ignored him. He spoke to the sergeant. 'Cuff him,' he indicated Ballinger, 'and bring him in!'

28

They removed the handcuffs. Left him stewing in an interview room. It was Penny and a female detective who finally entered. She introduced the DCI, and then herself as Detective Sergeant Ford. Then she went through the formalities with the recorder, announcing that Mr Ballinger had declined access to a lawyer.

'Thank you for helping us with our enquiries Mr Ballinger,' began Penny without a trace of irony. 'Perhaps you can start off by telling us about your relationship with the Shaws.'

'I don't have a relationship with them,' Ballinger said.

'You were found inside their home after someone reported a break-in.'

'I was found outside their home.'

'Lurking in the garden.'

'Looking in the garden. For Mr Shaw. With whom I had an appointment.'

'So you said. What did you want to see him about?'

'That's between me and him.'

'Not any more, it isn't. Frank Shaw was found dead this morning under suspicious circumstances.' The DCI studied Ballinger's face as he delivered this news.

Ballinger frowned. 'And you think I had something to do with that?'

Yes I do, Mr Ballinger. So, since you appear to be unwilling to tell me about this business you claimed to have had with Mister Shaw, perhaps you could tell me where you were yesterday afternoon.'

'Is that when he was killed?'

'Yesterday, afternoon Mr Ballinger? Where were you?'

'I was in Bristol, to begin with.'

'Bristol?'

'Bristol airport, to be exact.'

'From when?'

'Eleven forty.'

'That's very precise,' remarked Penny

'I was picking someone up. I mistimed the journey and got there fifty minutes early.'

'Who were you meeting?'

'Terry Dutton and his wife Alex. Oh, and a flying ambulance attendant.'

'I'm sorry?'

'Terry Dutton, of Abacus Investigations,' explained Ballinger patiently. 'He was hit by a car a week or so back, in Ulster.'

'Yes, I heard about that.'

'Well, they released him from hospital yesterday morning. I went to meet him and his wife.'

'And what time did they arrive?'

'Around twelve-thirty.'

'So then what did you do?'

'I went with them to their home, in Portland. I stayed for a meal. Then I left.'

'What time did you leave?'

'Some time after five.'

The conversation did not appear to be going the way

Penny wanted. He reverted to his earlier question.

'What was your involvement with the Shaws?'

'I told you, I am not involved with them. I have never met them. I called last week on a business matter and they were out. I left my card.

He, or someone claiming to be Shaw, called me on Wednesday. Told me to meet him at the house. I went there, but again there was no one in. I hung around for a while in case they had just slipped out, and then the police arrived. Look, if you don't believe me ask Mrs Shaw. She'll tell you we have never met.'

'I can't!' Penny said the words with a finality that spoke volumes.'

'Jesus!' This time Ballinger was taken aback. 'Her too? Both murdered?'

'I didn't say that!'

'You said 'suspicious circumstances.' Amounts to the same thing. Look, I'm sorry they're dead but I have never met either of them. So I really can't help you.'

'Yes you can. You can tell me why were you there?'

Ballinger shook his head. 'I can't answer that. Not until I've spoken to the person I was there to represent. So, unless you want me to fall back on the old '*no comment*' game, I suggest you stop asking me questions I have already declined to answer.'

Penny smiled. 'I've heard Dutton has been sniffing around the Carroll case?'

'Have you now? Well, I'm afraid you'll have to ask Mr Dutton himself if you want to know anything about his business. I'm not his business partner.

'But you are an associate?'

'The Duttons are friends of mine, DCI Penny,' smiled

Ballinger. 'A concept you may not be too familiar with. Can I ask you a question? Why, exactly, am I here?'

'You were seen acting suspiciously at the Shaw house some days ago,' stated the policeman. 'That makes you a person of interest.'

'I can see that. But you searched my home. Why? Did someone call crime-stoppers? Say they saw me making off with Shaw's lawn mower?'

Penny didn't answer. Ballinger threw out another question. 'Does the name Gerald – or Gerry – Dawson mean anything to you inspector?' He carefully watched the man's eyes as he asked, but they gave away nothing. Ignoring the question, the DCI climbed to his feet.

'Your problem Ballinger,' he lectured 'is that you are too clever for your own good. You are one of those people with an answer for everything, and a mouthful of attitude to go with it.'

'Are we done here?'

'You are free to go, for now,' Penny told him. 'But don't think this conversation is over because it is not. And don't think of taking yourself off to anywhere I cannot find you. Have you got that?'

Ballinger ignored the question. 'Do I get a lift home?' he asked.

'Call Uber!'

29

During the taxi ride home, Ballinger thought about the events of the day. Whatever decisions he and Dutton might have reached about the future of the Carroll investigation, were now irrelevant. Things had changed. The murder of the Shaws, and this attempt to lay the murder at his door, was a massive escalation of whatever game was being played out.

Ballinger had read many an entertaining tale about members of the intelligence services going rogue. Killing their own to keep their dark secrets hidden. But that was fiction. Surely the Security Services were not in the business of killing respectable citizens like the Shaws. If, indeed, they were respectable. Yet wasn't that just what Dawson was alleged to have been doing in Ulster? Setting up innocent people to be murdered by terrorists?

But regardless of who was behind the killings, the fact remained that a line had now been crossed. It was too late to walk away. He and Dutton could now expect far more direct moves to be made against them. Perhaps also, he thought uncomfortably, against the instigator of this whole thing, Roz Carroll.

Back in his study he called Dutton. Told him about his day. Promised to go down to Portland and discuss the implications of recent events.

Next, he called the journalist Mark Addyman.

'I hope this is good,' answered the reporter. 'I'm watching Gogglebox.'

'What do you know about two people being found dead today?'

'Well, just that!' he answered. 'Two bodies. Found after a tip-off to the police. Names withheld, pending relatives being informed.'

'It's the Shaws.'

'Who?'

'The people who live in the Carroll house.'

'You're kidding me! Bloody hell, Ballinger, how do you know that?'

'I've just been questioned by DCI Penny. It seems I am a 'person of interest!'

'Really? So, we are looking at murder, then?'

'Looks like it.'

'Well they were found in a derelict factory, slap bang in the middle of town. People don't visit derelict factories to commit mutual suicide, do they? Not when they have a nice comfortable home to do it in? Nor do the police pull in suspects unless they are looking for a killer. Why are they interested in you?'

'I've been trying to contact the Shaws about the Carroll enquiry. I was spotted at their house.'

'Did they arrest you?'

'They searched my home. When they found nothing, they took me in for questioning. When I told them I wasn't even in Dorchester yesterday, and could prove it, they let me go.'

'Where were you?'

'Where was I? You sound just like DCI Penny. If you

must know I was at Bristol airport, picking up Terry Dutton. He came home yesterday!'

'Really? How is he?'

'On the mend. But he has some way to go yet.'

'Well give him my regards. Oh, and thank you for the heads up on the Shaws. If you get any more information will you let me know?'

'I will. But hold on Mark, we're not finished yet. This is a two-way communications channel, remember?

'Go on! What do you want?'

'You – or someone in that newspaper office – will be researching the Shaws to put together an obituary. I could do with a copy of that.'

'They'll do a profile on them. But not until their names are released. Tomorrow, I would think. The quickest way to get your hands on that is from the online edition.'

'Okay,' voiced Ballinger. 'There is one other thing, and I know this is a big ask, but I need information about our friend Dawson. If he is still with the Service he will be protected, I know that. But if he is not, then I need to know what he is doing these days, and where he is doing it from. Addresses, phone numbers, the name of his dog? Anything you can get.'

'What makes you think I can get stuff like that?'

'You're the press. You can access sources that are closed to people like me. You've already demonstrated that. And if you can't do it yourself, I'm sure you'll know a man who can.'

'Are you saying that Dawson is involved in all this?'

'I don't know about the Shaws? But I am fairly sure he knows more about Michael Carroll's disappearance than He led everyone to believe. I'd like to ask him about that but first I need to find him, and right now I don't even know where to start looking. I'm hoping you can help me with that.'

'I'll do what I can,' agreed Addyman. 'But if it turns out he was withholding information about the Carrolls, I want to know about it. Not that he's likely to tell you.'

'You never know?' remarked Ballinger. 'I can be pretty persuasive?' He ended the call.

30

Tuesday. Week 3.

Alan Badell found himself wide awake. Staring into darkness. Normally a sound sleeper, he wondered what it was that had disturbed him. He sat up. Glanced at the luminous dial on the bedside table. One-fifteen. For a while he lay there, listening. But heard nothing. Probably late-night revellers. Or some noisy vehicle passing down the road.

He lay back down. Closed his eyes. He was just drifting off when a sharp metallic sound rang out, close by. He sat up, instantly. Seconds later he heard the noise again. It was coming from the workshop, below.

Cursing, he climbed from the bed. Switched on the light. He pulled on his jeans and sweater and slipped his feet into a pair of trainers.

Quite deliberately he dressed himself with as much noise as he could make. A former police officer, he had long since learned the dangers of attempting to tackle intruders single-handedly. If someone had broken into his workshop, he wanted to let them know they had disturbed him. That he was on his way down. Most burglars would flee, rather than be confronted by an angry victim.

Before leaving the room, he went to his wardrobe. He pulled open the doors and lifted a pitching wedge from his golf bag. Just in case.

Leaving the bedroom he approached the outside door. Turned on the hallway lamp and the bulkhead light that was outside, over the metal staircase. He turned the key, opened the door, and stepped cautiously onto the small, exterior, landing.

He looked down. No sign of anyone at the side of the building. Hoping the intruder had made himself scarce, he descended to the bottom of the stairs.

There was no one in the yard. He looked at the front of the building. The workshop doors stood open. With a sigh he approached the doorway. Using the golf club, he rapped noisily on the door frame. He waited. Nothing happened.

Cautiously he peered inside. The workshop and office were in darkness. Over in the far corner, a light was showing in the storeroom. Reaching inside he switched on the workshop lights and looked around. He saw no one. Gripping the wedge, he made his way towards the storeroom.

'You can come out!' he commanded as he neared the door. 'I know you're in there!' There was no response. He counted thirty seconds then decided it was safe to move. Golf club at the ready, he stepped quickly through the open door. Then stopped dead.

The storeroom was not large. Just a central walkway with Dexion shelves on either side, it ran for about twelve feet. At the far end, seated on the low step ladder he used for reaching the upper shelves, was a stranger. The man stared at him, blankly.

Not a burglar, thought Badell. Too well-dressed for that. Too old, and too well fed, too.

'Who the hell are you?' he asked the intruder.

The man's mouth broke into a mirthless smile. 'Well you took your sweet time getting down here,' he said, in a broad Ulster accent. 'We didn't think you was ever gonna wake up.'

'We – ?' Too late Badell felt the presence behind him. Before he had the time to react, the cold barrel of a gun was pressed into the nape of his neck.

'Put down the club, Alan,' said a voice. 'Or I will put a bullet in your spine.'

31

The call came in at 2-10am from a passing taxi driver. The Salisbury call centre immediately turned out the Lyme Regis watch. A second appliance was dispatched from nearby Charmouth, and a third from Colyton in Devon.

The local fire fighters were on the scene in just under eight minutes. They found the ground floor workshop well alight. The fire already making inroads into one end of the upper storey.

'What's upstairs?' asked the watch commander.

'Living quarters,' replied someone. 'The owner lives up there. Alan Badell. Used to be a copper.'

'Family?'

A shake of the head. 'Lives alone. Doesn't mean he can't have visitors, though.'

Whilst most of the watch began to tackle the fire, three fire fighters wearing breathing sets, made their way up the exterior staircase at the end of the building. Reaching the top, they quickly forced open the locked door.

Thick smoke poured out. The flames engulfing the other end of the workshop were given a new impetus by the sudden through draft.

The fire fighters pushed on into the smoke. Began checking the rooms that lay off what was more a corridor than a hallway. The first room was a bathroom-cum-toilet.

It was empty. The next door opened up into a bedroom. Lying in his pyjamas, on top of the bed, was a man.

One of the fire fighters went on to check out the kitchen and the lounge, further along. His companions dealt with the casualty.

Badell was on his back. His mouth was open, his eyes closed. When they tried to rouse him, he showed no signs of life. An empty whiskey bottle rolled to the floor as they lifted him from the bed.

They carried him out through the exit, passing two more fire fighters carrying in a hose to tackle the blazing lounge area. Once outside they were re-joined by their companion. With a shake of the head he indicated he had found no one else in the upper rooms.

The victim was carried down the staircase and into the yard. Laid on a blanket on the ground. The place was now a hive of activity with three crews tackling the blaze.

'Anyone else in there?' asked the commander.

They shook their heads. 'Did a visual. Apart from this fellow, it looks empty.'

One of the team was kneeling beside Badell, checking his airways. He searched for a pulse but found nothing. 'Not good!' he declared.

They began CPR. Were still working on him when the ambulance arrived. 'How long has he been like this?' asked the paramedic.

'We've been working on him for around ten minutes. He was like this when we found him.'

The paramedic took over the CPR. He sent his companion for a defibrillator. Four times the victim was given an electric shock. Four times his heart stubbornly refused to restart.

They gave it a further ten minutes but the man was beyond help.

'Alright, that's it,' sighed the paramedic, climbing to his feet. 'There's nothing more we can do for him. All agreed?'

'Agreed,' acknowledged the others.

32

By the time Ballinger knocked on Dutton's door the next day, more bad news had broken on local media.

'Badell is dead,' said Dutton, by way of greeting.

'What!'

'It was just on the news. His workshop burned down last night. They recovered a body. They're not saying it's him, but his flat was over the workshop.'

'This is not good, Terry. Where is Alex?'

'In town.'

'Perhaps you should get her back here. I think it's time the two of you dropped out of sight for a while.'

'What do you mean?'

'I mean, you need get away from here.'

'Are you kidding? We've only just got home.'

'Listen Terry, this is not a game anymore. People are dying. You stay here, and there is every chance you will join them.'

'And what about you?' argued Dutton. 'Are you going to run away and hide, too?'

'I can look after myself.'

'So can I.'

'No you can't! You are vulnerable. Right now, you couldn't protect yourself from a ten-year-old. And what about Alex? How would you protect her?'

'Oh come on, mate – '

'Terry when they come, they will come for both of you. Like the Shaws'

Dutton lowered his eyes. 'I'm going nowhere,' he repeated, but with less conviction. 'But you're right about Alex. Perhaps she should go away for few days.'

'And she'll do that, will she?' demanded Ballinger. 'Go off on her own. Leave you here to face whatever?'

'Probably not,' conceded Dutton. 'Look, perhaps it's time we told the police what we know.'

'And what do we know? All we have is a lot of suspicions and conjecture. You were a copper? Would you have acted on what we have?'

He tried again. 'Come on, Terry. We don't know who we're up against here. But it looks like we've panicked them into shutting things down. They're killing anybody who might have known anything. There is no way they are going to leave us standing.'

'What about Roz? Is she in danger, too?'

'Probably. But don't worry, I'll take care of Roz. Right now I need you and Alex out of here fast. To somewhere they can't find you. Jo should be warned, too. She needs to shut up the office and stay at home.'

Dutton thought long and hard. 'All right,' he conceded, finally. 'We'll go. But I want you to keep me updated at all times, on everything that is happening. And make sure you stay alive, or Alex will kill me. Okay?'

'Deal,' agreed Ballinger.

33

Roz Carroll left the Asda store carrying a bag for life. Inside were a pack of six, easy peeler clementines, a plastic container full of blueberries to mix in with her muesli, a bottle of water, and the reason she had gone to the store in the first place, a set of ink cartridges for her printer.

But shopping was not the only reason for the short journey to Weymouth. She had picked up a get-well card for Mr Dutton, to drop into to the Abacus office. Despite the phone call informing her that Terry was now home, and feeling much better, she still felt a great sense of responsibility for what had happened.

Sitting in the car she wrote out the card and then sealed it in the envelope. She wrote his name on the front, then drove off into the town centre.

Leaving the car on double yellow lines outside the office she darted across the pavement and dropped the card into the Abacus letter box. Back in the car she headed for the Dorchester road. She picked her way through local traffic, finally entered the relief road, and turned for home.

She settled down at a steady speed and glanced in the mirror. There was a big Mitsubishi close behind her. Too close, in her opinion. The black bodywork and wide grill loomed huge in her small, rear, window.

Gently she eased back, inviting the driver to pass. Annoyingly, he refused her invitation and slowed down with her. She increased her speed to put more space between them, hoping he would take the hint. He did not. Instead he put his foot down, maintaining the dangerously short gap between the two cars.

Peering through the wing mirror she tried to make out the face of the driver. It was a man, of course. His bulky torso was draped in a grey hoodie. His eyes covered by sunglasses. What little she could make out of his face appeared expressionless. Unsmiling.

Feeling slightly apprehensive, but mostly annoyed, she pressed her foot down heavily on the accelerator. Opened up a sizable gap between the cars. The man responded immediately. Within seconds he had caught up and was sitting right behind her again.

She dropped her speed down to twenty mph. Then down to fifteen. He did the same. Other drivers were now sounding off their horns, angrily, as they were forced to overtake the two slow-moving vehicles. She squirmed in embarrassment. Dropped her speed again. He must pass her. But he didn't.

They were approaching a long right-hand bend. Through the side mirror she spotted a group of four heavy vehicles coming up behind herself and her unwanted escort. At this speed, the convoy was quickly gaining on them.

Roz knew the road well. She increased her speed to match that of the convoy. Predictably, the driver of the Mitsubishi did the same. She maintained the same speed until she reached a half-mile layby sign, then she floored it. Her shadow followed.

It felt like a very long, half-mile. But at last the lay-by was opening up ahead. Without bothering to indicate she suddenly swung off the carriageway and slammed on the brakes, coming to an abrupt stop a few yards inside the parking area.

Caught out by the sudden manoeuvre, the driver behind was unable to follow her. Glancing sideways she was rewarded with the sight of a Mitsubishi Shogun shooting past. But her jubilation was short-lived. Some yards beyond the lay-by the Shogun screeched to a halt. The driver threw the large off-roader into reverse then, skittering slightly, he deftly backed the vehicle into the far end of the layby.

Okay, she thought. *Plan B.* A glance in the mirror told her the four-vehicle convoy was almost upon her. Jumping from the car she cast a quick glance at the Mitsubishi. The vehicle sat there, the engine ticking over. There was no sign of movement from the driver. Stepping to the edge of the carriageway she frantically waved down the approaching trucks.

The lead vehicle was moving too fast to stop. It drove by with a wave from someone in the passenger seat. The second vehicle also passed by, and the third. To her relief she saw the last of the trucks was already indicating, ready to pull in as it approached.

The heavy, camouflaged, military truck shuddered to a halt between the tiny Ka, and the Mitsubishi. The engine died and the driver and front passenger doors opened. Two men in army uniform climbed down. A sergeant and a corporal. They came towards her.

'Problem, luv?' asked the sergeant in his broad, northern, accent.

'It's him!' She pointed ahead to the Shogun. 'He's been tailgating me all the way from Weymouth. I speed up - he speeds up. I slow down - he slows down. Ten miles an hour I took it down to, and still he wouldn't overtake. Sat right behind me, as close as he could get. Playing some weird game.'

The men looked at each other.

'Wait there,' said the sergeant. 'We'll have a word.'

The two men moved towards the Black Mitsubishi. But as they strode past their own vehicle, the Shogun suddenly came to life. The engine roared, the vehicle pulled quickly onto the highway and sped away.

The soldiers watched it disappear into the distance. Then they came back to Roz.

'I think he got the message,' grinned the corporal.

'Where're you going?' asked the sergeant.

'Dorchester.'

'That's not far. You can tag along behind us if you want, though I don't think you'll have any more trouble with that one.'

'Thank you for scaring him off,' she told them.

'No probs!' shrugged the sergeant.

Soon they were back on the road. A reduced convoy, with the tiny Ka tucked in behind the army truck. They trundled along at a steady fifty. When she reached her turn off, she flashed the headlights as a thank you. The truck's hazard lights flashed once in response, then it was lost from sight.

Feeling more relaxed she drove through the streets of Dorchester. As she approached a junction, she glanced into the mirror. Her blood froze. The Shogun was back. The half-hidden, implacable, face staring at her.

The surge of fear was suddenly replaced by a tide of anger. Up ahead she saw the façade of a local sports shop. She knew the place well. Used to buy tennis rackets and other sports equipment from there when she was at school.

There were double yellow lines on the road, but she didn't care. She pulled in, jumped from the car, and ran into the shop. A backward glance saw the Shogun pull in behind her.

Just inside the shop doorway stood an ancient wooden tub. It had been there for as long as she could remember. It was used to display second-hand bats and rackets that were for sale.

She snatched a rounders bat from the tub. 'Back in a minute,' she told the woman behind the counter then she was outside again.

The Mitsubishi sat four feet behind the Ka with its engine running. Advancing purposefully she bore down on the vehicle, lifted the bat, and with a mighty swing slammed it against the front passenger window. The glass exploded into a million fragments.

'Get out!' she screamed at the figure inside. 'Get out you pervert, to where I can see you!'

Taken aback by both the physical and verbal attack, the man hastily threw the Shogun into reverse. It shot backwards, hitting the front of a UPS truck that had just pulled in. Without signalling it then swung out into the line of traffic, almost took out a motorcyclist, and sped off into the distance. Roz was left by the kerb, bat in hand, fragments of glass clinging to her clothes and hair.

As the red mist began to dissipate, she became aware of the people around her. Pedestrians, some looking like they could not believe what they had just witnessed. Others who quickly, and nervously, averted their gaze from this wild-looking, bat-wielding, young woman.

Reaction kicked in. She began to tremble. Tears were just moments away. She needed to get away from here before she made a further spectacle of herself. But she could not move. Then someone gently took the bat out of her hand. A comforting arm was slipped around her waist.

'Let's go inside shall we, dear,' said the owner of the store, kindly. 'See if we can't get all this glass off you!'

As she allowed herself to be led away, a young mother holding a child's pushchair began to applaud her. 'Nice one girl!' she called out as Roz was ushered from the pavement, into the sanctuary of the store.

34

Alex proved to be more open to the idea of a few days away. She felt that after all she and Terry had been through, a few days away would do them both good. After a search on the internet, she booked them both into a health spa in Norfolk. A place where Terry would be able to enjoy a programme of specialised exercises, and physio.

'Physio!' he grumbled to Ballinger. 'Thanks, pal.'

Later Ballinger watched them drive away with packed suitcases. Then he set off for home. He was just the top side of Dorchester when his phone went. It was a number he recognised. 'Yes Roz?'

'I need to see you.'

'Now?'

'If you can, please.' She sounded troubled.

'What's wrong?'

'I don't want to talk about it on the phone.'

'Where are you?'

'At home.'

'I'm on my way.'

He turned around. Headed for the Wharton house. When he got there the door was opened by a man he presumed was Eddie Wharton.

'I'm John Ballinger,' he introduced himself. 'Roz is expecting me.'

The man waved him in. Showed him into a sizable lounge. There was a woman sitting on a settee, reading a book. The teacher, he remembered. The TV was on, but no one was watching it. The woman muted the sound as he entered.

'Mrs Wharton,' nodded Ballinger.

Roz sat at a dining table in the back of the lounge. She was playing with her phone. She looked up when she heard him and climbed to her feet. She lifted a jacket from the chair back and slipped it on. Headed for the door.

'That was quick!' she said to Ballinger. 'Come on.'

'Roz!' said the woman, throwing her a worried look.

'It's okay,' the girl reassured her. 'We won't be long.'

Ballinger followed the girl outside and they both climbed into his car.

'Where are we going?' he asked.

'There's a pub off London Road. Up near the Dinosaur Museum. It's not far.'

She gave out directions as he drove. 'How long have you been drinking?' he asked, conversationally.

'Started when I was sixteen. We all did. Doesn't have the same appeal once you can drink legally, though, does it.'

'It doesn't,' agreed Ballinger, remembering his own first beer at the age of fifteen.

Soon they were entering the pub. It was quiet. A man and a woman sat at the bar, nibbling nuts and drinking lager. In the lounge a couple of pensioners were putting the world to rights. They seemed in no hurry to drink the half pints of beer sitting on the table before them. He ordered a glass of coke, with ice, for himself, and a lager for Roz. Carried them to a corner table.

'Thank you,' she said. 'How's Mr Dutton?'

'He's okay. Be a while before he's back on the golf course. But he'll get there.'

'I called at his office today with a card for him,' she began, conversationally. Then she paused, gathering her words together. 'Last week,' she began, 'when I spoke to his receptionist, Jo, she told me you were a security consultant. Is that right?

He nodded. 'Sort of.'

'Does that mean you advise people on security?'

'Sometimes.'

'Good. Because I think I need some of that advice at the moment.'

She lifted the glass. Downed half the contents.

'Looks like you needed that?'

'I did.'

'So, what's happened?'

She told him about her drive up from Weymouth. She spoke quietly, dispassionately, like she had told the story several times already. She probably had.

'It was awful,' she said when she was finished. 'I was a mess. Everyone staring at me like I was some kind of lunatic. Anyway, the lady from the shop took me into her kitchen. Made me a cup of tea.' Her eyes glinted with tears. 'My mum used to do that. Said it made everything look better. I never believed her.'

'It's therapeutic,' he told her. 'Gives you time to get your head back together.'

'Well it worked! When I felt better, I told her what had happened. Why I smashed the car window. She was so nice and sympathetic. Called him an evil sod and said she would have done the same thing.

Someone must have called the police. The van driver, possibly. Anyway, two policewomen came into the shop. I thought they'd come to arrest me, but they hadn't. I had to tell the story all over again.

They were quite nice, really. Sympathetic. They asked if I needed medical attention, which I didn't, then they followed me home to make sure I was okay.'

Ballinger regarded the girl with new respect. She had shown remarkable coolness and courage during what must have been a terrifying ordeal.

'What did they say about him?' he asked.

'Probably some weirdo with a thing about women drivers. They checked my webcam for his number plate. Hopefully, they'll find him. I certainly don't want to see him popping up in my rear-view mirror again.'

'I don't think he will. Not after what you did. People like him are looking for victims. Someone they can terrorise. Not someone who fights back. I think you handled it just right.'

'Can I ask you something?' she said

'Go one.'

'Afterwards, I began to think about what had happened to Mister Dutton, and the Shaws – you've heard about them, right?'

'I have,' he nodded.

'I began to wonder if these things were connected. If it was all to do with me trying to find out what had happened to my mum and dad and Tony?'

Roz Carroll was no fool Ballinger decided. 'Listen,' he began, carefully. 'I have no answer for what happened to the Shaws. These things happen to some people and more often than not, the reason why it happened lies close to home. Besides, we don't know all the circumstances yet, so I think it's a little early for that kind of speculation.

But regarding the question of someone putting the frighteners on Terry, and now on yourself, you could be right about that. These two things could well be linked.

Terry and I had a meeting this morning,' he told her. 'It's going to be a while before he is fully recovered from his injuries, and that makes him vulnerable. So, to avoid any more 'accidents' he and Alex have decided to go away for a few days. Just to give me time to find out what's going on. In view of what just happened to you, my professional advice is that you do the same thing.'

'You think I should go away?'

'Until we know who, or what, is behind all this, yes I do.'

'But where would I go?'

'How does London sound?'

'Sound's great. But not on my own.'

'Don't worry,' he smiled, 'you won't be on your own.'

35

Back at the Wharton house he called his sister. Explained what he was asking of her, and why. He was not surprised when she agreed to help. He spoke to the Whartons whilst Roz was packing her case. Reassured them that she would be safe at his sister's house. That he himself, would be keeping an eye on her.

'London,' he told them, 'is the perfect environment to help her forget what she had just been through.'

They didn't want her to go. He could see that. But they didn't try and stop her. Probably knew they'd be wasting their time. Roz was quite a head-strong young lady.

She promised to call them every day and hugged them both. Then she and Ballinger left Dorchester, taking the A31 towards Southampton and London. They made good time. As he drove, she talked again about the Shaws.

'I know it sounds mean,' she said, 'but I never liked them living in our house. I used to go there, you know. Just sit outside, thinking about the way things used to be. Sometimes he would come to the window and wave at me. I know he was only being friendly, but I didn't like it. I wanted to go in there and tell them to get out of our house.' She was silent for a while. 'But I am sorry they are dead. What do the police think?'

He shook his head. 'It's early days. Perhaps they had enemies. What did they do for a living?'

'They worked for the local Council. She worked in the library. I've seen her there. I'm not sure what he did, but I know he's retired.' They drove on in silence, a moment or two. 'Are you sure your sister won't mind you dumping me on her?' she asked.

'I spoke to her. She's okay with it. My niece is home for summer. You'll like Charlie.'

'Charlie?'

'Charlotte. But everyone calls her Charlie. She's at university studying law. Just finished her first year.

'What does your sister do?' she asked.

'She's a barrister.'

'And her husband?'

'He's a high court judge.'

'I've never met a judge!'

'You haven't missed much.'

Joining the M4 they headed for London. Passed Heathrow and drove into the city. At Chiswick the M4 became the A4 and they continued onwards, before turning off for Kensington.

The De Havillands owned a country house in the Cotswolds, close to the village of Minchinhampton. The house stood on the edge of the common that bore the same name as the village. They rarely stayed at the house. Spent most of their time in the Capital, working out of a four-bedroomed maisonette in Kensington.

'Wow!' mouthed Roz as he pulled up before the Victorian terrace. 'You said a flat? This isn't a flat, it's a mansion. They've probably got servants and a butler, and everything.'

'They wish,' he said, climbing from the car.

'If I don't like it, can I go home?' she suddenly asked, a little nervously.

He smiled. 'Roz, you can go anywhere you want whenever you want, as long as you let me know you are okay. But this is London. The big city. If I were you, I'd make the most of it.'

The door was opened by Charlie who had been waiting for them. 'Hello uncle John,' she greeted him.

Ballinger accepted the hug. 'Just drop that *uncle* bit young lady, or you and I will be having a few words.'

'Sorry,' she smiled. 'Mum says I have to call you Uncle John while I'm living under her roof.'

'Let you off then,' he smiled. He introduced the girls to each other.

'Come on Roz,' Charlie said, brightly. 'I'll show you your room.' The two girls headed for the stairway, his niece chattering animatedly. Ballinger made his way down the hallway and descended into the basement.

He crossed the snooker room, with its full-size table. Entered the study. Maggie was sitting in a dressing gown before a computer. A glass of red wine sat beside her and an unlit cigarette dangled from her mouth.

'Thought you were giving those up?' he said.

'I am! I've been sucking this thing like a dummy, for days. But I'm damned if I'm going to light it.'

'Thanks for doing this Mags.'

'A bit more notice would have been good. How long will she be staying?'

He shrugged. 'A few days? A week? I don't know. I just want her out of Dorchester for a while in case this lunatic comes after her again.'

'He's not going to show up here, is he?'

Ballinger shook his head. 'No one followed us here. I made sure of that. So, unless he's a clairvoyant he won't know where she is.'

'What is she like?'

'I'm no expert on teenagers but she seems a nice enough kid. She's had it rough, though. First with her parents, and now this. I told her she needs to forget about Dorchester for a while. Go somewhere she can let her hair down and have a good time.'

'Well she's in the right place for that. Charlie will be glad of the company. Are you staying overnight?'

'I can't. Have to get back.'

'Have you heard from the Inland Revenue?'

'Not yet.'

'Good! Let's hope it stays that way.' She turned back to her computer. 'Sorry, but I need to get this ready. I'm in court in the morning. Don't forget to say hello to Donald before you go.'

'Where is he?'

'His den.'

'Okay, I'll do that now. Thanks again, Mags.'

She waved his thanks away and he walked from the study, leaving her to finish her paperwork.

36

Wednesday. Week 3

Ballinger sat in his study drinking coffee. Reading the obituaries on Frank and Helen Shaw. As Roz had said, both had spent much of their working life employed by the local Council. She as a librarian and he in the Registrar's office. He could find absolutely nothing questionable about their lives.

Today he felt more relaxed. With the Duttons in Norfolk, and the girl in London, he had only himself to worry about. What he needed to do now was make something happen. Provoke these faceless people into action, in the hope they would reveal themselves.

When his phone rang it gave him the perfect way of doing this. The caller was the journalist, Addyman.

'Gerald Dawson left the service one year after the Carroll's vanished,' he began. 'He is founder and CEO of a company called Sword Edge Security. They specialise in top drawer commercial, and cyber, security systems. They have Government contracts and have also done work for a slew of financial institutions, in the City of London. He has an apartment in Lancaster Gate, near Hyde Park.

Ballinger wrote down the address as the journalist read it out. 'Phone number?' he asked.

'Sorry, not available. You'll have to call him at the office. The number will be on the Company website.'

Ballinger thanked the man. Closing the phone he looked up Sword Edge Security on his laptop. The company operated out of a two-storey glass building on Nine Elms Lane. Not too far, he noticed, from the Intelligence Service's headquarters at Vauxhall Bridge.

The Company profile gave out lots of information for potential customers. Ballinger ignored this. He clicked on the *Management Structure* link. Found a pyramid chart listing the Company's personnel. There were none of the usual thumbnail mug shots to go with the names, but Dawson sat at the apex of the pyramid as CEO.

He returned to the list of services offered by the Company. It was impressive. Now he knew where the expertise to disable his home security system had come from. When he had seen all he wanted to see, he called the company's number. Asked the switchboard if he could speak to Gerald Dawson.

'I'm sorry, Mr Dawson does not have an office at SES. Can someone else help?'

'Do you have a contact number for him?'

'I'm afraid not, sir.'

'Can I get a message to him?'

'I'm not sure? Just hold the line, sir, and I'll put you through to Mr Palmer.'

Nigel Palmer, according to the chart, was the Company Secretary. He came to the phone, obviously having been briefed by the switchboard.

'Hello Mr Ballinger. Can I ask you what your business is with Mr Dawson?'

'That's strictly between myself and Mr Dawson,' replied Ballinger. 'But it is important. I'm sure he'll want to return my call.'

'Then I'll give your number to his secretary,' Palmer promised. 'But I must tell you that Mr Dawson is now semi-retired and spends much of his time out of the office. He may not get back to you for some time.'

'Mr Palmer just tell Dawson that I called again to discuss the Michael Carroll case. He will know exactly what you are talking about. Tell him I will continue to call until I have an answer from him,' and with that, Ballinger shut down the phone. He did not expect to hear back from Dawson. But hopefully, the man would be rattled enough to react.

Finishing his coffee, he moved into the barn. Spent most of the day working on the car, waiting for something to happen. The work was both therapeutic and time-consuming. By the time he had reached a convenient point to call it a day, it was early evening.

Back in the house he called Roz. 'How is it going?'

'I like Charlie,' she told him.

'Thought you might. What do you think of London?'

'I haven't seen much of it yet. Tomorrow we are off sightseeing. It'll probably rain.'

'Doesn't matter. There are lots of indoor things to see and do. Just enjoy yourself. If you need to speak to me, call me. Anytime, okay?'

'Will do,' she promised.

He checked his watch again. Then called his old friend, Colin McKay.

'Hi Col!'

'Sandy! How's it going?'

'I was wondering if you had turned up any names for me yet?'

'I am struggling, my friend. It's not that no one left the

province around that time. People were always jumping ship. It's finding someone who fits the profile you gave me. I've put the word out over there, so you never know. Someone might get back to me with a name. But right now it's not looking too good.'

'There is something else you can help me with,' Ballinger told him. 'I'm trying to narrow it down in time. We know that Michael Carroll was living with his mother, in Ballymena, in nineteen ninety-eight.

We also know that at some point during that year she became terminally ill, and she passed away at the end of September. After this he left the province.

My guess is that he carried on living in that house, until the day he sailed. Assuming he was liable for the rent and Council tax, then he would have paid both right up to, and including, the date he left the property.'

'And you want to know that date?'

'His landlord would have kept records. They might still be there. Also, the local Council will have records of when the Carols stopped paying Council Tax on the property.'

'What if he didn't leave straight away? What if he moved in somewhere else for a while before he left?'

'I don't think he did that. According to his local newsagent, Carroll couldn't get away fast enough. So, I'm betting that as soon as he buried his mother and tied up the loose ends, he was out of there on the first available ferry to the mainland. But even if he did hang around for a day or two, it would still narrow things down a lot.'

'Okay, give me the address. I know some people in Local Government. I'll see if I can get it checked through their records. As for his landlord, he may well be retired, or dead, even. So unless the rent was collected by an agency that is still in business, any records from that time will be long gone. But I'll do my best with the Council, and as soon as I know something, I'll get back to you.'

'Thanks Col. I owe you.'

'No you don't.'

37

Ballinger made himself a coffee then opened up his computer. He typed in Joseph Maguire, the name of the rogue accountant McKay had mentioned, the day he called to see him. Several Joseph Maguires came up, but he soon found the one he was looking for.

The last known sighting of Maguire was October seventeenth, 1998, when he boarded the ferry at Larne, bound for Stranraer in Scotland. Three years later, in July 2001, his car was pulled from a Scottish fishing loch. What was left of Maguire's body was still in the driving seat.

A provisional identification of the body was made from items found in the car. This was later confirmed by the Police Force of Northern Ireland when DNA samples, taken from the body, proved to be those of the missing Belfast accountant.

An inquest brought in a verdict of unlawful killing, and the man's remains were cremated. The missing person case and the fraud enquiry were closed, and a murder case was opened. It remained unsolved.

Ballinger widened his search. Studied accounts from local newspapers that had covered the incident. The loch in question was close to the town of Newton Stewart, in Dumfries and Galloway. Joe Maguire's remains were discovered when the loch was being drained.

Few details of the investigation were given in the press, and the story was short-lived. A follow-up piece on the inquest verdict appeared some weeks later in the Galloway Post:

Like the investigation before it, the inquest on missing accountant Joseph McGuire has been taken out of local hands. Yesterday, after a closed inquest in London, a verdict of unlawful killing was announced. The nature of this inquest reinforced speculation that this whole business touched on some aspect of National Security. It appears that the bemused members of the Tannside angling club will now have to wait at least fifty years, possibly longer, to learn just who it was dropped this poor fellow and his car into their loch, and why? The author of this piece was a journalist called David Moss.

Ballinger looked up the *Galloway Post*. It was a rural newspaper that started up in Newton Stewart in 1954 and closed down in 2005. He went through the telephone directories for the Newton Stewart area. There were two listings for David Moss.

He called the first number. A woman answered. 'Mrs Moss?' he asked.

'It is.'

'Sorry to trouble you, but I'm trying to contact a David Moss who used to be with the Galloway Post.'

'That's my father-in-law,' she informed him. 'My husband is David junior.' She gave him another number to call. He tapped it in.

Moss himself answered. Ballinger told him he was with Abacus Investigations of Weymouth. That he was seeking information about the sunken car incident at the Tannside fishing loch, back in 2001. He asked if they could meet up.

Moss agreed to meet in his local pub at noon the next day. 'I'll tell you what I know,' the man said, 'which isn't much. But in return, I'll want to know what your interest is. I might be retired, but I'm still nosey.'

When Ballinger ended the call, he checked the time. It was seven pm. He had an eight- hour drive ahead of him. He packed his overnight bag and placed it in the car.

He stripped off the clothes he was wearing and showered. Then he dressed himself in clean jeans and tee-shirt, and a short leather jacket. He ate a slice of ham and egg pie, only two days past its use-by date, and washed it down with diet coke. Then he locked up, climbed into the car, and set off.

38

Thursday. Week 3

Sometime before three a.m. he checked into the Travel Lodge near Dumfries. Falling into bed he slept until eight. By nine-o-clock he was driving along the A75 towards Newton Stewart.

Halfway there he pulled into a garden centre near Castle Douglas for breakfast. Then he was back on the road. Soon he was driving across the river Cree, into the town centre. Half a mile down the busy road he spotted what he was looking for and pulled in.

Leaving the car, he ducked inside the Galloway Angling Centre. Minutes later he was back out, carrying a hastily drawn map. He turned the car around, then headed out of town the same way he had entered.

Back on the A75, he soon found the narrow road that was indicated on the map he had been given. The road climbed for half a mile before he came to the gravelled lane, off to the right. He turned into it.

The narrow, single, track had passing places, every fifty yards or so. It ended abruptly at a wide turning circle, close to a fenced-in wooded area. To his left was a stout, wooden, gate with a notice bearing the legend 'Private Property: Tannside Angling Club.'

Ballinger left the car in the turning circle. He approached the gate. It was bolted, but not locked. Sliding back the bolt he pushed his way into a gravelled parking area that sloped away gently, towards the loch.

Casually he strolled down to the water's edge. Gazed across the tree-shrouded expanse of water. It was very still. Barely a ripple disturbed the mirrored surface. Unable to resist the compulsion, he picked up a handful of gravel and threw it far out, over the water.

What he found most interesting about the loch was its location. Just off the busy highway that ran from Stranraer to all points east and south. Close enough to the road to make a speedy getaway, if needed. Far enough away to make it the perfect place for an execution. A well-chosen spot, he thought.

He walked back up the slope and entered the toilet. Swilled his dirty hands with cold water. As he rubbed them dry on a coarse paper towel, he heard the sound of a car. The gate complained noisily as it was pushed wide, then the sound of wheels on gravel confirmed he was no longer alone. Casually he strolled outside.

An ancient, silver-grey, Volvo estate car stood in the car park. A man climbed out. Elderly, he stood ramrod straight with the bearing of someone who had spent years in the military. His face bore a look of confident authority that Ballinger recognised at once. Top brass, he decided. You couldn't fake it.

'Are you a member?' asked the stranger by way of greeting. The voice held just a hint of Scottish brogue.

Ballinger shook his head. 'Tourist.'

'This is private property. It says so on the gate, which you left open by the way.'

'Sorry!' offered Ballinger with a disarming grin. 'Hope I didn't let any of the fish out.'

The man was not amused. 'It's no laughing matter. That gate is there to keep out the sheep. Stop them crapping everywhere. What are you doing here?'

'Just following my nose. It's what I do. I'm a photographer. I look for interesting places off the beaten track. This is a nice spot you have here.'

'We like it,' observed the man.

Ballinger tilted his head towards the water. 'Correct me if I'm wrong. Isn't this the place where they found a body in a car, some years back?'

The man's eyes narrowed. 'It is. But we don't advertise it. Nor do we want the place turned into a tourist attraction. So I would rather you did not take any photographs.' He gestured towards the gate. 'In fact, I think you should leave.'

'No problem,' said Ballinger, pleasantly. 'I was just going, anyway.' He strode away, watched by the man.

'Close the gate as you leave,' ordered the man.

Ballinger stopped. He turned. Gave the man a long, expectant, look.

'Please,' added the stranger, belatedly.

Ballinger gave him a small salute. He pulled the gate shut, bolted it, and climbed into the car. After shunting it around he set off slowly back down the lane. Through his mirror he saw the man leaning on the gate, writing something down on a piece of paper. His number plate, probably.

39

Back in the town he pulled in outside the Galloway Arms. As he made for the door a slim, elderly, man with a freckled forehead and thinning ginger hair, stepped forward. 'Mister Ballinger?'

'Right first time, Mister Moss,' Ballinger shook the offered hand.

The two men entered the pub. Ballinger bought the drinks. Moss made no attempt to offer.

'You drove up here from Dorset?'

'Overnight!' Ballinger told him. 'I've been doing some sight-seeing. It's nice around here.'

'It is. But then it's nice in Dorset, too – in a different way. You don't sound Dorset,' observed the man. 'You sound more like someone from across the water.'

'Long time ago,' Ballinger told him.

Moss took a long swig of beer. 'So, what are you looking for up here that you couldn't ask me about over the phone?'

'I told you. I have an interest in the body that was found in the loch.'

Moss said nothing. He sat, waiting for more.

'Alright,' Ballinger went on, 'I'll tell you what I can. I am searching for a man who disappeared some years ago.

Vanished from his home for no apparent reason. He, too, was originally from Ulster, and he left there at around the same time as your Joseph Maguire. I was wondering if there might be a connection between the two?'

'Well, there's no one else in that loch, if that's what you're thinking. It was drained completely back then. Are you saying the two men might have been travelling together?'

'It's a possibility.'

'When did he disappear, this fellow?'

'Six years ago.'

'Six years? That's a long time after McGuire was killed. You'll have to work hard to link one man's death twenty-odd years ago, to another's disappearance just six years back.'

Moss downed more beer. 'But you are right in one respect,' he continued. 'The day Joseph McGuire died, he was not travelling alone. He may have thought he was, but he wasn't. He was travelling with his killer. But then I could have told you that much over the phone.'

Ballinger smiled. 'You could. But it's not the day he died that I am interested in. It's the day he was found. You must have been here that day. Covering the story. So you'll know everything that went on. Your article implied there was some kind of cover up by the authorities. So why don't you tell me what brought you to that conclusion.'

Moss swallowed the rest of his beer. He held out the empty glass and looked expectantly at Ballinger. 'Come on, laddie.' He said, tapping his head. 'It'll cost you more than a pint to get what's inside here!'

Ballinger took the glass. 'Same again?'

The man nodded. 'Aye. Wi' a clean glass and a whisky chaser, if you please.'

Ballinger went to the bar. He collected the drinks and carried them back to the table.

'Will you be going up to the loch?' asked Moss.

'Been there. This morning. I was thrown out by some military type who acted like he owns place.'

'Driving a Volvo?'

'That's him.'

'Hugh McDonald. Brigadier McDonald, formally of the Black Watch. He does own the place. The loch sits on his land. He's the patron of the club.' Moss picked up the replenished glass. 'Cheers,' he offered, taking the top off the beer. 'Okay then, I'll tell you what I know. You can make of it what you will.

It started with dead fish,' he began. 'Something was killing off the fish in the loch. The club called in the local Council. They sent someone up here to collect fish and water samples. These went to the Environmental offices in Dumfries, and tests showed that the loch was contaminated with petrol.

The first thought was sabotage. Animal rights people were making noises about angling, around that time. Also, some local feminist group was trying to stir up trouble about the club's 'men-only' stance.

Anyway, whoever, or whatever, had caused the problem, the club now had a decision to make. If they wished to continue fishing, which they did, then the loch would have to be drained, decontaminated, then refilled and re-stocked.'

'A big job,' offered Ballinger.

'A major task,' agreed Moss, 'and expensive. But with

financial help from the National Environment Agency, and donations from several of the local businesses, work began three months later. It was a lengthy business. The loch is surprisingly deep. The water had to be pumped out into bowsers then taken away to be safely disposed of. But, little by little, the water level went down.

Three weeks into the project, the source of the contamination was discovered when the roof of a car broke through the surface of the receding water. The job immediately came to a standstill, and the police were called in.

When police divers entered the loch to examine the car, they discovered the remains of a body in the driving seat. The victim's wrists were bound, and there was a bloody great bullet hole here –' he placed a long finger against his forehead, 'right between the eyes.'

'Next morning a crane arrived and pulled the car from the water. A tent was erected around it, and police forensic teams moved in.

In the late afternoon the police announced that the car, and the items found inside it, pointed to the victim being the missing Ulster accountant, Joseph Maguire. A preliminary examination indicated that the victim had been kneecapped, and then shot in the head. The body was taken away, and a murder enquiry was launched.'

Moss paused to take a drink. Then continued. 'You can imagine that we journalists were all pretty excited about this. Here we were in sleepy Galloway, where the most serious criminal investigation in years had been about discovering who stole old Mrs Keegan's milk from her doorstep, and we finally had a real murder mystery on our hands. One that looked good to run for weeks.

But it didn't work out that way. At ten-o-clock the next morning, whilst we all waited for the next chapter of this thriller to begin, all activity suddenly ceased. We watched in astonishment as the police teams packed up all their gear, then went away. Leaving behind just a couple of uniforms to guard the scene.

One of these, Sergeant Murray, was a local lad. He told us that the County boys had been ordered off the crime scene by the Home Office. That anti-terrorist officers were on their way up from London to take over the investigation.

Sure enough, later that same day these 'supposedly' anti-terrorist police arrived. The first thing they did was throw a cordon around the loch. Pushed us all back down to the road. Then their boss told us that the crime scene was now a National Security issue. That the Home Office had imposed a news blackout, so we might as well all go home.

Most of us ignored this and stayed put. Bloody-mindedness, I suppose. Later that evening we all watched the car being taken away on the back of a pick-up truck. We were not happy. They were stealing our murder.

At seven-o-clock the next morning, Maguire's body was quietly taken from the police morgue in Dumfries. It was placed in a hearse and driven south to London, along with every piece of evidence found. By lunch time, less than twenty-four hours after they'd arrived, the whole circus was on its way back to London. No press release! No nothing.

A week later, with still no information coming out of London, the police in Belfast announced that DNA samples had confirmed that the body found in the loch was indeed that of accountant Joseph Maguire. There was no public inquest, so the whole thing became the story that never was. Hidden away by the Security Services.'

'Hang on, you said the anti-terrorist police. They are not part of the security service.'

'And if that lot were policemen, then I'm the Pope,' growled Moss. 'According to Sergeant Murray, their boss was some bigwig called Dawson. We looked him up. Dawson was no policeman. He was a spook. Got himself kicked out of Ulster for causing all sorts of problems.'

'Let's be clear on this,' asked Ballinger. 'Are we talking about Gerald Dawson here?'

'The very same, laddie. The very same.'

40

Ballinger sat in the Forton services, just south of Lancaster. He was on the phone to Dutton. Filling him in on what he had learned. 'Two possibilities here,' he began. 'Either someone took Maguire there, executed him, then hid his car and body in the loch?'

'Or,' put in Dutton, 'Maguire took someone to the loch. Killed him. Then left his own papers with the body so that if it was found, everyone would think it was him.'

'Could have happened either way,' Ballinger agreed. 'The body was whisked off to London so quickly that no one else had a chance to examine it. It could have been anyone in that car. But if the SIS were hell bent on closing the McGuire case, that body turning up gave them the perfect opportunity to do so, don't you think?'

'Are you thinking it was Michael Carroll in the car?'

'It would fit. McGuire kills Carroll. Then steals his identity and sets up a new life for himself with the stolen money. The only problem with that scenario is the DNA evidence that put McGuire in the car.'

'Might be worth trying to find out if both men were on the same ferry that night?'

'I'm already working on that. I've got Colin McKay trying to pin down Fallon's departure date from rent and Council records.

'There might be another way.' Dutton told him. 'There must be archived passenger lists filed away somewhere. Do we know who was running the ferries back then?'

'It was Stena! I used them myself when I was stationed over there. They still operated as Sea Link, sailing between Belfast and Stranraer, which is about half an hour up the road from where the body was found.'

'Convenient!'

'Very.'

'Where is Stenna's UK base?' asked Dutton

'I have no idea!'

'Neither have I.'

'Got any better ideas then?'

'Leave it with me,' said Dutton. 'Those records must be out there somewhere. Genealogists use old ship's passenger records for tracing the movement of people's ancestors. I'll make some enquiries. Give me something to do when I'm not on the physio's rack.'

'Okay, but keep a low profile,' said Ballinger ending the call. He finished the coffee then returned to his car to continue his journey.

By the time he reached Sherborne it was dark. He turned from the road onto the farm track that led to his house. It was a bumpy ride. The unadopted lane was little more than a dirt track, used by heavy farm machinery.

Once he had passed the farmhouse, the surface became bumpier still. The car see-sawed as he navigated, by memory, around the worst ruts and potholes. Not for the first time he promised himself that someday, he would have the whole lane gravelled over.

He was approaching a sharp right-hand bend with a particularly deep pothole just before it. Automatically he swung the wheel over to avoid the hole. As the car lurched sideways, a bullet hole appeared in the windscreen. The bullet passed through the space where his head had been a moment ago and exited through the tailgate window.

He instinctively ducked down behind the wheel as another bullet screamed over his head. Followed by a third. Ballinger flicked off the car's lights and kept the car moving. Using the side window, and the looming dark form of the hedgerow as a guide, he followed the bushes around the curve as they fell away to his right.

Another bullet struck the side of the car. Then he was through the bend, with the lane opening up ahead. Sitting up, he floored the accelerator. Fishtailing wildly, the car leapt forward. He ducked involuntarily as a fifth bullet struck the back of the car, hitting something that rang like a bell.

Approaching the house, he spun the wheel and pulled on the hand break. The back end of the car slewed through ninety degrees, and he drove into the gap between the barn and the house where he came to a stop.

Jumping out he opened the side door of the house and entered the kitchen. He unlocked the gun cupboard and removed the shotgun. Grabbing a box of shells he loaded the gun, slipped a few shells into his pocket, then ran outside. He took cover behind the barn.

He was not about to go in search of the shooter. For all he knew, his attacker might have a night scope on his rifle. But from where he was standing, he would hear anyone approaching the house, either along the lane or across the back field, long before they saw him.

Time passed. He heard no one. After forty minutes he relaxed and went back inside the house. Collecting a torch, he climbed into the field. Strode past the rear of the barn and walked along behind the hedge, parallel with the lane. He came to the spot where the would-be assassin had lain in wait.

The smell of firearms discharge lingered in the air as he peered through the man-made hole in the hedge. He found himself looking up the lane towards the farm. A perfect place for a head-on shot. But for the hole in the road, that first shot would have killed him.

It occurred to him that had the lane been gravelled, he would now be dead. There was a moral there, he decided. Never do today what you can put off until tomorrow. It might just save your life.

Satisfied the shooter was gone, he returned to the house. He locked the door and put away the gun. Pouring himself a whiskey he downed it in one. Then he refilled the glass and sat there. Thinking, ruefully.

He had been hoping that Dawson would react to his telephone call in some way, and that wish had been granted. He just hadn't been expecting such a rapid, and lethal, reaction as the one he had got.

41

The girls stepped from the theatre their heads full of music from the show.

'What do you think?' asked Charlie.

'Wicked,' laughed Roz, unable to resist the pun.

'I said you'd enjoy it. I still can't believe you've never seen the Wizard of Oz. It's been on television every Christmas since forever.'

'I never really fancied it!' confessed Roz. 'I always thought Judy Garland was, like, ancient history.'

Charlie laughed. She looked at the line of cabs waiting by the roadside. 'I think most of these will be booked – no, wait a minute, there's one!' One of the drivers was signalling he was free.

They hurried forward. Before they reached the cab, the door was pulled open by a heavily made-up woman who looked suspiciously like a man. 'Sorry darlin'!' the driver told her, 'I'm already booked.'

With a small gesture of frustration the man, or woman, drifted away and the girls climbed in.

'Cheeky blighter,' grinned the driver. 'Where are we going, ladies?'

Charlie gave him the address. The driver closed the sliding window and set off. The girls sat back giggling about the cross-dresser.

'There's lots of them in London,' Charlie said. 'They have their own clubs and everything.'

'Have you ever met any?'

She shook her head. 'I don't think so. But then you wouldn't necessarily know, would you?'

They chatted on about the show. Roz was telling Charlie that the one and only time she had ever been to London was when she, and her parents and brother, had come up to the West End to watch *Les Misérables*.

'You must miss them terribly,' sympathised Charlie. 'I don't know what I'd do if I lost my mum and dad.'

'I do miss them,' voiced Roz, wistfully. 'At first, I thought about them all the time. But not so much now. I suppose I've got used to them not being around. Does that sound awful?'

'Not at all! I think it's awesome, the way you've moved on with your life. I'd still be in pieces. I think your parents would be really proud of you – ' Charlie stopped talking as something outside the window caught her attention. 'Hang on, where's he taking us?' Addressing the driver, she called out. 'You're going the wrong way, driver.'

The cab driver took no notice.

'I said, you are going the wrong way!' she called out, louder this time and rapping on the partition.

Still the driver ignored her.

Charlie was growing angry. 'What are you doing?' she demanded, loudly. 'You are going the wrong way. Stop this cab, now, and turn around!'

The driver pulled into the side of the road. Turning round, he slid open the partition window and rested the barrel of a gun on the seat top. 'Okay, girls, take out your phones!' he demanded.

They looked at him, eyes wide in disbelief. Roz was the first to recover. 'Get lost!' she voiced, making to open the door. It wouldn't open. When she looked back the driver was pointing the gun at her.

'Phones now!' he ordered. Still the girls hesitated. He raised the gun. His voice grew harder. 'Come on, they're only toys! They're not worth getting hurt for.'

Reluctantly the girls took out their phones.

'Let me see you turn them off,' he ordered. The girls complied. 'Now, put them into your handbags and let me have them.' Silently the girls dropped the phones into their bags and passed them over. The bags disappeared into the front of the cab.

'Thank you' said the man. 'Now, just so you know, I am not going to hurt either of you, so you don't need to go into panic mode. Best you just sit back and enjoy the ride, as they say. Oh, and don't bother trying the doors or windows,' he added. 'They won't open from the inside.'

He slid the window shut. Moments later they were back on the road, heading up the A4. 'Do you think that's a real gun?' asked Roz, quietly.

'I'm not sure I want to find out,' replied Charlie.

It was late. There was little traffic on the roads. The chances of attracting anyone's attention were slim. They tried waving desperately at passing vehicles, mouthing the word 'help' but they got no response. All anyone saw were two drunken girls on their way home from a night out, pulling faces at them from the back of a cab.

By the time they joined the M4 out of the city the girls had stopped trying to catch the attention of other road users. Instead they sat there, forlornly, faces etched with concern. Huddled together for mutual comfort.

'I don't believe him,' whispered Roz, 'about not harming us. No one goes to all this trouble just to steal a couple of handbags and mobile phones.'

'So, what do you think?'

'I don't know. But whatever he has in mind, he has to let us out some time. When he does, we can jump him. I've done Karate, and there are two of us.'

'What about the gun?' asked Charlie.

'It might not be real.'

'But what if it is?'

Roz had no answer to that.

42

The cab drove on. It left the M4 and joined the M25 but didn't stay on it long. Soon they left the motorway and took a road that stretched away into the darkness of open countryside. There was no traffic around. The driver put his foot down for several miles, before turning into maze of narrow lanes.

Eventually they came out onto a long, straight, road with not another car in sight. After a couple of miles the cabby finally slowed and pulled into a layby.

He climbed out. Left the engine running. Gun in hand he pulled open the door next to Charlie.

'C'mon darlin' out you get!' Charlie didn't move. The man raised the gun. 'Don't make me use this, sweetheart. Just get out or I'll put a bullet in your leg and drag you out.'

The girl still didn't move. 'What are you going to do?' she asked, nervously.

'Nothing,' spoke the man. 'I'm not interested in you. So come on, get out!'

Charlie turned her head and looked at Roz. Roz squeezed her arm and nodded. 'You go, I'll be all right.'

'No you won't!' Charlie turned back to the man, shaking her head. 'I'm not leaving my friend!'

Without warning the man reached in. Grabbing hold

of Charlie's long hair he pulled her down from the seat, dragging her backwards out of the cab. With her legs still inside the vehicle he let go of her hair and she fell, heavily, onto the road. The back of her head struck the road surface with a sickening impact, and her world dissolved into darkness.

With the gun trained on Roz, the driver reached in and cautiously lifted Charlie's legs clear of the vehicle. Then without a word he slammed the door shut and climbed back into the cab. He put the cab in gear and drove off up the road.

Some miles further on, he turned into a winding lane. After a short ride the taxi pulled into the yard of a derelict farmhouse and stopped. He switched off the engine, but he didn't move. He lit a cigarette and sat there, waiting.

It started to rain. From time to time the cabbie checked his watch, but he said nothing. When Roz tried to engage him in conversation, he told her to shut up. So she did.

An hour went by. Then twin beams of light lit up the farmyard, announcing the approach of another vehicle. The cab driver climbed out and watched the new arrival pull up alongside.

Roz's felt her heart sinking. Even in the darkness she recognised the black Mitsubishi Shogun. The two men exchanged words. A package was handed over to the cab driver, then the taxi door was pulled open.

The newcomer leaned into the back of the cab. He smiled unpleasantly. 'Hold out your hands!' he demanded. Roz did as she was told. Her wrists were bound tightly with cable-ties. 'Come on, out you get! And don't do anything stupid.'

She slid along the seat. Swung her legs out of the cab. Stepped down onto the slippery, wet, cobbles. The stranger gripped her arm so tightly it made her gasp. He steered her through the rain to the back of his car. He opened up the tailgate, pulled her around to face him, then pushed her down into the boot.

He turned her into the foetal position then secured her ankles with another set of ties. As he was doing this Roz heard the taxi drive away.

She had not thought it possible to feel more scared than she already did. But as the sound of the taxi faded, a cold, dark, despair settled upon her. Irrational though it was, the presence of the taxi driver had given her some reassurance. Now she was completely alone with this man.

When he was sure she was secure enough, her captor took a box from his pocket. He opened it up and took out a syringe. Flicking off the cap, he squeezed a little liquid out of the needle then plunged it into her arm.

'No!' she cried.

The man ignored her. He emptied the syringe then removed it. Placed it back in the box. 'You're going to sleep!' he told her, with a strong Irish accent. He leaned forward and looked into her eyes. 'I once met your old fella, you know,' he told her. 'I've been looking forward to meeting you.'

She heard the words, but their meaning slipped away into nothingness, along with her consciousness.

Some miles back, Charlie came to her senses. She was lying on her back, looking up at the night sky. For a moment she wondered where the bedroom ceiling had gone. Then she suddenly remembered.

'Roz!' She sat up and was instantly overwhelmed with dizziness. Leaning over she retched violently, but with little in the way of food in her stomach, her mouth filled only with bile.

She waited for the giddiness to pass, then looked around. She was sitting in the road beside the empty layby. The cab was gone. Roz with it. Frantic with worry for the fate of her friend, she considered her options. She needed to find a phone so she could call home and speak to her mum. Her mum would know what to do. She always knew what to do.

Slowly she climbed to her feet. Her head hurt like hell. Every movement threatened to bring back the dizziness, but she knew she couldn't stay where she was. She had to find help.

She set off walking. There was nothing behind her for miles. So she headed out in the direction their captor had been driving. There might be houses ahead. Soon it began to rain. Then pour. There was no shelter here. Not even a tree to stand beneath.

She stumbled on, through the rain. Each step a major effort. She could barely stand, let alone walk, and when her left foot suddenly sank into a hole, she went face down onto the sodden grass, the world spinning around her. She did not see the lights of the car approaching from behind. Nor did she hear it pull in alongside her. By the time the driver reached her side she had slipped back into unconsciousness.

43

Friday. Week 3

The phone rang. Ballinger was just out of the shower, towelling himself down. He stepped into the bedroom and picked up the phone. It was his sister.

'Hi Mags?'

'The girls didn't come home last night!' she blurted out. 'They went up the West End to see a show, and they didn't come home.' For the first time in his life Ballinger heard the sound of panic in his sister's voice.

'When did you find out?'

'Just now. Normally they would be home by eleven. But if they were calling for something to eat or drink, it might be later. We were in bed for ten-thirty, so it wasn't until this morning that we realised they had not come home.'

'Did you try their mobiles?'

'The first thing we did. They are both switched off. We're worried sick!'

'Have you called the police?'

'Donald's on to them now.' There was a pause. 'John, I hope this has nothing to do with something you are involved with?'

'I honestly don't know?' he told her, knowing that it almost certainly was. 'Look Mag's, just sit tight,' he told her. 'I'll be there as soon as I can.'

He dressed himself quickly, then put on his riding leathers and boots. The car was full of bullet holes so he would have to use the bike.

Carrying crash-helmet and gloves, he entered the barn. The bike stood in the corner, covered by a tarpaulin. Taking off the cover, Ballinger wheeled the Honda CTX outside. Donning helmet and gloves, he locked the barn door and started up the bike.

Halfway to London he pulled in and checked his phone. There was a message from his sister. He called voice mail.

'John, it's me. They've found Charlie. She is in hospital, but she is okay. I don't know about Roz. We'll probably know more by the time you get here.'

He texted back a brief acknowledgement then continued his journey. When he finally arrived in Kensington, he found four marked police cars in front of his sister's home. He left the bike by the roadside and headed for the building. He was stopped at the door by a uniform.

'Where are you going, sir?' He was asked.

'I'm Mrs De Havilland's brother. John Ballinger. She's expecting me.'

The cop made a call to someone on his radio then waved him through.

Inside the maisonette were still more police. Two uniforms and two detectives.

'Thank god you are here,' said his sister. 'Let me introduce you.'

She led him across the room to where Donald was talking to the detectives. Ballinger and De Havilland nodded a greeting to each other.

'This is Detective Chief Superintendent Groves, and DI Meadowcroft,' she introduced the two men. 'This is my brother, John. He'll be able to tell you about Roz.'

The Chief Super shook his hand. 'That's John – ?'

'John Ballinger,' he told the detective. 'So, what's happening?'

'Miss De Havilland has been found,' the senior officer informed him. 'She was admitted to the Royal Berkshire hospital early this morning with head injuries and concussion. She was found unconscious by the roadside, near Waltham St Lawrence. She had no identification on her, so it wasn't until she woke up this morning that anyone knew who she was.'

'What about Roz?'

'She has not yet been found. The local police are out there now, searching the area. But we don't know whether Miss De Havilland was knocked down, or if she fell, or jumped, from a vehicle. Until we have spoken to her, we won't know what happened.'

'I understand Miss Carroll recently had problems with a stalker,' put in Meadowcroft.

'That's right,' Ballinger told him. 'She was followed from Weymouth to Dorchester by a man driving a Black Mitsubishi Shogun.'

'Was the incident reported to the police?'

'It was. Roz was interviewed by two policewomen at the time. She was quite upset, and her confidence was badly shaken. She came to London to get away from Dorchester for a while. Try to put the incident behind her.'

'What is your relationship to Miss Carroll?' asked the Chief Super.

'I'm sort of working for her.'

'In what capacity?'

'It's a long story,' sighed Ballinger.

Groves turned to DI Meadowcroft. 'David take Mr Ballinger down to the car and get his statement, will you. Do you mind, Mr Ballinger?'

Ballinger did mind. But he didn't say so.

'John, you can use my den,' offered De Havilland.

Ballinger thanked his brother-in-law then led the Inspector to the den.

It took an hour to give the Inspector a full statement. With Roz missing, this was no time to be shy. He started with the disappearance of the Carrolls. Moved on to the current efforts to learn their fate, initiated by Roz and pursued by Terry Dutton and then himself.

He was closely questioned about the attack on Dutton, the deaths of those on the periphery of the enquiry, and the alleged attempt by others to implicate him in at least one of these deaths.

He didn't mention the evidence planted in his house, or his visit to Scotland and the attempt on his life. Nor did he voice his doubts about the real identity of Michael Carroll, and his suspicion that an ex-member of the intelligence community was somehow involved. He didn't want anyone talking to Dawson before he, himself, had the chance to.

'How much of this have you told the police in Dorset?' asked the detective.

'Are you kidding? I wouldn't tell DCI Penny his trousers were on fire. He'd try to fit me up for it. I think everything that has happened, including the kidnapping, is linked to the disappearance of the Carroll family. But I doubt Penny would choose to see it that way.'

'It does sound a little like a Lynwood Barclay novel,' suggested Meadowcroft. 'But I will take your concerns seriously, Mr Ballinger. Firstly, because two young women have been abducted – one of them the daughter of a high court judge – and I am sure you can imagine how that piece of news went down when it reached the top floor.'

'Which is why I thought she'd be safe here,' said Ballinger. 'I mean, who would be stupid enough to kidnap the daughter of a judge, and her friend?'

'Anyone come to mind?'

Ballinger shook his head. 'Not yet.'

'But you're working on it?'

'I'm thinking about it.'

DI Meadowcroft nodded. He rose from his seat. 'Alright Mr Ballinger, that's all for now. I'll be in touch with Dorset to get their take on this. Meanwhile, if you do come across any information that might be useful to us, please call me.' He handed Ballinger a card. 'Remember, our resources are far better than yours.'

'So I've heard,' muttered Ballinger. 'Oh, Inspector?' he called out as the policeman made for the door.

Meadowcroft turned. 'Yes?'

'You said *firstly*. What other reason did you have, for taking my concerns seriously?'

Meadowcroft eyed him for a moment. 'We've met before,' he said, 'though I doubt you'll remember me. I was at Hereford when you came back from Northern Ireland. You were something of a legend, back then.'

Ballinger nodded. 'One of the lads, were you? Well, you shouldn't believe everything you hear about people?'

'Oh I don't Mr Ballinger. I wouldn't be much of a copper if I went around doing that, would I?'

After speaking to Meadowcroft, Ballinger called the Whartons to tell them what had happened. It was not a call he was looking forward to. But he didn't want them hearing the news from the police or the media. It was Mr Wharton who answered the phone.

He broke the news as gently as he could. Told the man that the police were even now launching a massive operation to find Roz. Assured him that she would soon be found.

Wharton was distraught. And scared. Scared for Roz. Scared by what the next few hours, or days, might hold. He wanted the name of the police officer in charge of the operation. Wanted to know what steps were being taken to find Roz. Ballinger gave him Groves name. Told him he was the high-ranking officer in charge of the search.

Wharton was not reassured. His anxiety turned to anger. Directed, mostly, against Ballinger himself.

'We shouldn't have let her go with you,' he said, accusingly. 'You said she'd be safe, so we trusted you. Now you're telling me she is missing. Kidnapped – or worse! Well, so much for your promises.'

'We will get her back, Mr Wharton. I promise you.'

'Don't make more promises you won't be able to keep,' replied the man, scathingly. 'It's the police we have to rely on now. Put this Superintendent on the line, will you: and don't call us again unless you have some good news to tell us.'

'I hear you, Mr Wharton. And I really am sorry. Do you want me to call your wife and tell her what has happened?'

186

'No, I do not!' returned the man angrily. 'You've done enough.'

Ballinger returned to the lounge. He passed the phone to Groves then retreated to one of the armchairs. He understood the man's anger. He was no less angry with himself for his failure to protect the girls. What had happened was his fault. He had made the cardinal error of underestimating the enemy. Because of that his niece was lying in a hospital, and Roz was almost certainly in the hands of a killer.

When Groves had finished speaking to Wharton, Ballinger called Dutton. He described the events of the last few hours, taking personal responsibility for what had happened.

'Best not to start with the blame game,' he was told. 'That won't get us anywhere. Seems to me that had you locked her up in the Tower of London and swallowed the key, they would still have found a way to get to her. That's some operation they just pulled.'

'They're running rings round us,' sighed Ballinger. 'Every time we feel we might be getting somewhere, somebody throws in a grenade. Perhaps it's time I threw in one of my own.'

'What are you going to do?'

'I'm going to find Dawson. I'm getting tired of playing catchup all the time, so I'm going to go round to his place and kick his door in. Then he and I are going to have a long chat.'

'You can't do that! You'll be arrested!'

'I doubt it. Dawson is in this up to his neck. There's no way he can risk involving the police. When I've spoken to him I'll tell you what he says.' He passed on the details of the investigating officers to Dutton, then he closed down the phone.

His sister entered the lounge.

'We're going to the hospital to see if we can bring Charlie home,' she told him. 'Are you coming?'

He shook his head. 'I'll stay here,' he told her. 'Give her my love, will you. If she asks about Roz, tell her not to worry. Tell her I'll find her.'

'John, you really need to leave this to the police. There is nothing you can do!'

'She's right,' advised the Chief Superintendent. 'Leave this to us, Mr Ballinger. We'll get her back if anyone can.'

You might, thought Ballinger, *but will she still be alive?*

44

Roz slowly came round. It took some time for her head to clear enough for her to work out that she was still in the boot of the car, and that the car was moving.

She was covered by something that smelled vaguely sweaty and felt like a duvet. Her body was cramped, and the floor of the car was hard and uncomfortable.

With nothing else to do, she began taking note of whatever information her senses were giving her. The constant, high-pitched, whine of the car told her it was moving fast. There was no slowing down, braking, or gear changing so she reasoned they were on a long, straight, road. Possibly a motorway.

This was borne out by the sound of other vehicles being overtaken, and then falling behind. There was no discernible sidewards motion, such as you get changing lanes, so she guessed they were, indeed, on a motorway. Speeding down the fast lane, overtaking other cars.

With no sense of direction, or of how long she was unconscious, she had to accept she could be anywhere in the country by now. Almost certainly miles away from where anyone would be looking for her – if indeed anyone was looking for her. Hopefully, Charlie would let people know what had happened. But the last time she saw her friend, she was lying unconscious in the road.

Recalling what had happened to Charlie made her fearful. Terrifying visions of what lay ahead when they arrived at their destination, added to her despair. She began to cry, her body wracked with sobs. She did not fight against the wretchedness enveloping her. She felt she was entitled to feel this way. Better to cry now and get it done with, she decided, than to show weakness to her captor.

She must have cried herself to sleep. She found herself experiencing a series of vivid dreams. In one she was running, bare-footed, along Chesil beach, holding high a beautiful blue and gold kite. She was trying to get the kite airborne, but however fast she ran over the hard pebbles, it wouldn't take off.

Then a great, blustery, wind came in off the water, lifting the kite high into the sky and taking her with it. For long minutes she hung there. Gazing down upon the sea and the beach, with a sense of great exhilaration. Then suddenly the kite was gone, and she was hurtling towards the ground at a terrifying speed.

The falling sensation snapped her awake. Moments later her senses told her something had changed. The constant motion of before was gone. Now the car was moving through gears occasionally. Speeding up, then slowing down. They must have left the motorway. The car was moving more slowly, in busy traffic.

She thought of calling out. Screaming aloud in the hope that someone would hear her. But she knew enough about cars to remember they were designed to be as sound-proof as possible. The only person likely to hear her screams was the man sitting behind the wheel. There would be no help from him.

An idea crept into her head. She might not be able to tell anyone where she was. But she could at least let them know where she had been. She remembered films and books in which kidnap victims had left clues to their whereabouts for others to find. She doubted it would save her, but it was better than doing nothing.

She turned onto her knees. Rested her forehead on the floor of the boot and lifted her bound hands until they connected with the chain around her neck. Slowly she worked it over her head until the weight of the Ankh pulled it off. It fell to the floor of the boot.

Scooping it up with her fingertips, she worked it into the palm of her right hand. Then she resumed her former position, keeping a tight grip on the trinket.

Soon, the car began to slow. The indicator lights blinked, then the car turned off from whatever road it had been travelling along. For a minute or two it drove steadily. Then it turned again, before finally coming to a halt. The ignition was switched off. Seconds later the boot was raised. The cover was pulled from over her.

'Out you get,' ordered the driver.

She struggled to sit up, blinking at the bright daylight. Impatiently the driver pulled her up into a sitting position.

'Swing your legs out,' he ordered.

'I can't move them,' she complained. 'They've gone numb.'

The driver went to the front of the car and Roz took a look around. They were in a private yard, in front of a big house with no other properties around it.

When the man returned, he was carrying a Stanley knife. He leaned in and cut the ties around her ankles. Pocketing the knife, he reached down to lift her legs over the sill. As he gripped her ankles, she launched her bound fists at a spot just behind his ear.

The fists connected solidly with his neck. He reared backwards with a sharp cry of pain. In an instant she rolled her body out of the boot. Her feet hit the floor, but her legs were too cramped to carry her. She went down, hitting her head on the car's rear bumper.

Roughly the driver pulled her to her feet. Pins and needles raged through her lower limbs and she clung to the car for support. He swung a vicious back-handed slap across the side of her face. Would almost certainly have given her more of the same, but at that moment the house door was opened, and another man came out.

'Stop messing about and get her in here!' ordered the newcomer.

The driver pushed his face close to hers. 'You'll be sorry you did that, bitch,' he promised. Then he closed the boot lid and pulled her, stumbling, towards the house. Six feet from the threshold she let the ankh and chain slip from her hand.

45

Lancaster Gate was on the Northern edge of Hyde park. About a mile away from South Kensington. Ballinger left the bike outside his sister's apartment and walked. Once he was through the park, he soon found the four-storey apartment block that Gerald Dawson called home.

Approaching the front entrance he studied the intercom. Four buttons for four apartments. A full floor per apartment. Dawson was on the top floor. He pressed the button. He knew he was being videoed, but he was past caring. Seconds passed and no one answered. He tried again. Still no answer.

He peered through the glass doors, into the foyer. To the left, a shelf ran along the wall, at waist height. Above the shelf sat a row of mailboxes. He moved his finger and pressed the button for apartment number three.

'Hello?' said a cheerful, female voice.

'I have a delivery for Gerald Dawson?' he said.

'Number four!' she told him.

'I know. He's not in. I can leave it in reception. It's only stationery.'

'I'll buzz you in.'

'Thank you.'

The door buzzed. Ballinger pushed his way through, into the foyer. To his right was the door for apartment number one. Further along was an elevator door. Beyond this a third door carried a plastic sign reading STAIRS.

Ballinger ignored the elevator. Probably key operated, anyway. He entered the stair well and climbed to the top floor. Stepping into a hallway, he made his way past the elevator to Dawson's front door.

It was pretty solid looking, and it boasted an expensive-looking multi-lever lock. He pushed against it experimentally to test its strength. To his surprise it swung open. 'Curiouser and curiouser,' he muttered.

The door had been left on the latch by the last person to use it, the key left in the keyhole inside. He stepped into a short hallway, dimly lit by light from a small window with vertical blinds.

'Dawson!' he called out. 'Gerald Dawson!'

Silence.

He opened the inner door. Stepped into a large lounge with two wide windows along one wall. Ballinger glanced around the room. Sparsely furnished, two white leather armchairs sat facing a wall-mounted television, and in one corner of the room stood a small bar, shaped like a ship's prow. Very retro, he thought.

The only other piece of furniture in the room was a baby-grand piano that sat before one of the windows. The lid was up, the keys uncovered. Not just for show, then. He wondered if Dawson himself played.

Ballinger moved to the window. He was looking out across the park. Not too many views like this in London.

There was a framed photograph perched on the sill. It showed a man and a woman, both dressed in tee-shirts and shorts. They stood holding hands and smiling, posing before a rather grim-looking country house.

Moving from the lounge he stepped into an open plan kitchen-diner. He was impressed. The place was fitted out with just about everything that Ballinger had never had, plus some.

Finding no one in there, he returned to the lounge. He crossed to another door and opened it. It led into a windowless hallway with doors leading off. Two of these opened up into spacious bedrooms. A third into a wet room that smelled of shower gel.

Facing him, at the end of the hall, was a fourth door. On it was stuck a small ceramic plate that showed a little boy in a plaid kilt, urinating against a tree. Below the picture were the words *The Wee Room*. He pushed the door open.

Sprawled face down over the toilet bowl, was the body of a man. The wall behind the toilet was spattered with blood and tissue. Rivulets of blood had run down, to pool on the top of a slimline cistern. At just about head height, one of the wall tiles was pierced by a single bullet hole.

Carefully he checked the body. Rigor mortice was fully set in so Dawson, and there was no reason to believe this might be anyone else, had been dead for at least twelve hours. Sometime yesterday, probably.

Ballinger grimaced. This was not what he needed.

Leaving the body where it was, he retreated to the lounge. Just for a moment he considered walking away. But this would only lead to him being hunted down and arrested as a suspect. He'd had enough of that.

With a long sigh, he pulled out his phone and the card that DI Meadowcroft had given him. Then, before he had time to change his mind, he called the number.

46

'**So tell me** how you just happened to be inside Gerald Dawson's apartment?' asked DI Meadowcroft. They were seated inside an interview room, attached to Scotland Yard's Murder Squad offices.

'I went to see him,' answered Ballinger.

'How did you get into the building?'.

'Wasn't difficult,' shrugged Ballinger.

'Obviously not. I suppose you conned your way in, using the old delivery scam?'

'Like I said – '

' – It wasn't difficult?'

'No.'

'So much for security,' noted the policeman. 'Go on!'

'I went up to the apartment and found the door open. I called out, but no one answered. So, I went in for a look.'

'Why?'

'It seemed suspicious.'

'In what way.'

'Well come on, the man runs a security company. Can you see him popping down to the local off-license, and leaving his door open?

'Okay, so what happened next?'

'I couldn't find anyone. So I went looking. I found him in the loo.'

'Dead?'

'Very!'

'Were you surprised he was dead?'

'More disappointed than surprised. I needed to talk to him.'

'About what?'

'He was the Intelligence liaison officer on the Carroll case, five years ago. I was looking for any information he might have had.'

'And what about the kidnap and disappearance of Roz Carroll, last night?' asked the detective. 'Did you think he might have information about that?'

'Had I found him alive, I might have been able to answer that question. But the chances are he was killed before the kidnapping occurred. That's not to say he didn't know about it, of course. He may well have been involved in organising it.'

'What makes you think that?'

'Come on, Inspector. Two girls step out onto a crowded footpath in London's West End and just vanish. No reports of any disturbance. No ransom phone call. Then one of them is left lying by the roadside, way out in the sticks, while the other one is spirited away.

A job like that has security service written all over it. Dawson worked for them for years. He was a field officer in Ulster, during the troubles. He would have no problem setting up an operation like that.'

'Why are you so sure he was involved?'

Ballinger leaned forward. 'Because every time we lift a stone, we find the name Gerald Dawson written underneath it. And one thing I have learned about Dawson is that he was not a man of action. He preferred setting up targets, then sitting back and letting others do the dirty work.'

'Why didn't you tell me all this before?'

'I should have, and I probably would have, after I had finished questioning him.'

'What would you have done if he had been alive when you got in there?'

'I would have systematically broken every bone in his body until he told me where Roz Carroll is.'

'Then his being dead saved you a measure of embarrassment, didn't it?' suggested Meadowcroft. 'And in case DI Wrexham asks that same question when he interviews you, I suggest you give him a slightly different answer to the one you just gave me. In fact, just stick to wanting to ask him about the Carroll family's disappearance and forget about the kidnapping. That way you might not give him cause to try and link you to yet another murder.'

'DI Wrexham? Who's DI Wrexham?'

'Murder squad! He'll be investigating Dawson's murder.'

'Oh? I thought you were – ?'

Meadowcroft stood up. 'No! I am dealing with the kidnappings. I just needed to know why you were after Dawson. What connection, if any, you thought he had to last night's events. Thank you for sharing that with me. At last!'

'Sorry!' said Ballinger. 'Present company excepted, I tend not to get on very well with police officers.'

'Or Revenue officers, I hear. Now before I go, is there anything else you know, or suspect, that might help me find that young woman?'

Ballinger shook his head. 'I'm as much in the dark as you are.'

'But that won't stop you looking, will it?'

'If I knew where to look, no. But right now, I don't even know where to begin. Dawson was the only lead I had.'

Meadowcroft studied him closely. 'Listen, Ballinger, I have a great deal of respect for what you were. But that is all in the past. If I find out one more time that you've been keeping things from me that might help me do my job, I will have no alternative than to come down on you like a ton of bricks. Have you got that?'

Ballinger nodded. 'Got it!' he nodded.

Taking Meadowcroft's advice Ballinger told the murder squad detectives he had gone to see Dawson as part of the Carroll investigation. He told them he had called Dawson's office for an appointment some days ago, and that he was still awaiting a reply. So, whilst in the area, he had gone to the apartment hoping to find Dawson at home. None of this was far from the truth, anyway.

Before being released he had to subject himself to a firearms residue test. This didn't bother him. He knew it would come out clear. They also took his fingerprints for elimination purposes. This did bother him. They told him the prints would be destroyed when the investigation was closed. He did not believe them.

Back in South Kensington he discovered Charlie was home. He badly needed to speak to her, but his sister told him she was in shock and refused to let him near her. Not looking for an argument he said he would speak to her on the phone later. Then, with nothing more he could do in

London, he climbed into his leathers and set off for home.

When he arrived back in Dorset, he approached the house with extreme caution. But this time there was no gunman lying in wait. Once inside the house he removed his boots and leathers, poured himself a whiskey, and then called Addyman.

'I have something for you,' he informed the journalist.

'Go on?'

'It's not exactly local news, but Gerald Dawson is dead. Murdered!'

'Bloody hell! When did that happen?'

'Sometime in the last twenty-four hours. He was found dead in his apartment today.'

'This is getting scary, Ballinger. You are getting scary. People are dropping like flies, all around you. I hope this is a secure phoneline we are on?'`

'It's a burner.'

'Good! So, what happened to Dawson?'

'Someone shot him in the head – and you didn't get that from me.'

'Don't worry Ballinger. As far as the rest of the world is concerned, I've never heard of you. I'm not in any hurry to join your dead fans society. Do you think his murder is linked to the others?'

'Has to be, hasn't it?'

'Then keep me in the loop, will you. Especially if something local breaks.'

'Will do.' Ballinger closed the phone. The fact that Addyman had not mentioned the girls, was good. It meant the police were keeping a lid on the kidnapping.

Having spoken to one reporter he decided to call another. He rang ex-Galloway Post reporter, David Moss. 'Thought I'd let you know,' he told him, 'Dawson is dead. Someone killed him.'

'You're kidding me?'

'Shot to death in his own home.'

'Hells bells? Was he still with the Service?'

'He retired some years ago. Ran his own Security Company.'

'Not a very good one then, was it? Did you get a chance to speak to him?'

'Been too busy,' Ballinger told him. 'Now I never will.'

'How is your investigation going?'

'One step forward, two back. People keep dying on me.'

'Well good luck anyway. And thanks for letting me know.'

His next call was to Dutton. He spent half an hour talking to his friend. Bringing him up to speed. Then he poured himself another drink.

Sitting down, he went through everything in his head. Looking for something he might have missed. When the exercise yielded up nothing new, he finished the whiskey and went to bed.

47

Saturday. Week 3

DI Meadowcroft looked up as the Chief Super entered his office. It was rare to see the boss in the building at weekend. But this enquiry was still being closely monitored by those upstairs.

'How's it going?' asked Groves.

'Some progress, sir,' the Inspector told him. 'We have video from the front of the theatre that shows the girls getting into a cab. Unfortunately, according to the PNC the cab does not exist. It is carrying false number plates, and a false hackney licence plate. But we did get a half decent shot of the driver's face.

According to Miss De Havilland, the cabbie locked the passenger doors so the girls could not get out. He confiscated their phones at gunpoint then drove them out of London. She was then dragged from the cab, after which he took off with her friend.'

He looked at the senior officer. 'He's done this before sir. Brighton, Dover, and Luton. Usually he picks up a lone woman, takes her phone at gunpoint so she can't call for help, then drives to somewhere quiet, where he rapes her. And those are just the three we know about. There may be more. We are contacting other police forces for similar reports.'

'How long does he hold them?'

'Normally just as long as it takes him to do his thing. Then he dumps them and drives away.

'But it's been, what, nearly thirty-six hours since the Carroll girl was taken? So where is she?'

'That's what bothers me, sir. Either this time he's holding onto the girl – '

' – or something else has happened to her,' finished Groves. He turned to leave. 'Okay David, Stick with it. Let's hope it's the former and she turns up alive and well. He hasn't killed anyone yet, has he?'

'Not that we know of sir.'

Minutes after the chief left, a perfunctory knock on his door announced the arrival of Meadowcroft's detective sergeant.

'Nothing in from anywhere else yet,' reported the sergeant. 'This feller could have been at it for months, Guv. A lot of rape victims don't report it. We're putting his face out on the News this evening. That might stir things up a bit. Until then it's a waiting game.'

'Where would someone who is not a cabbie get hold of a black cab?' asked Meadowcroft.

'Believe it or not, Guv, you can actually buy a used cab on ebay. Then there are companies who trade in second-hand cabs – not to mention auctions.'

'Another dead-end then. What about the other car? The Mitsubishi that followed the girl home.'

'Ah! That one is registered to a Vet. He runs a rural practice near Chelmsford. Says he's been nowhere near Weymouth, or Dorchester, for years. The day the girl was harassed he was using the Shogun all day. Visiting local farms, testing cattle for TB. He has no end of witnesses, and certificates that he issued, to prove it.'

'So that's another car running around on false plates. Who does that, except a criminal?'

'Someone who gets his kicks going around scaring women-drivers, I suppose. But that doesn't make him a kidnapper, Guv? Especially with our taxi driver friend moving nicely into the frame. But there was one thing?'

'Go on.'

'After we put the Mitsubishi's registration number out on the system, we got a hit from an ANPR camera on the M6, up in Cumbria.'

'Cumbria? And it wasn't the Vet?'

'Definitely not.'

'What's he doing in Cumbria, I wonder?'

'Spot of mountain climbing,' grinned the sergeant

'Yes, well put it out as a stolen and pass it on to Cumbria Traffic. He's either a thief or a menace, or both, and he needs taking off the roads.'

'Will do.'

As the sergeant left the office, Meadowcroft reached for the phone.

48

The first thing Ballinger did after breakfast was call Charlie. His intention was just to ask how she was. But she obviously wanted to talk about her ordeal, giving him chapter and verse from when she and Roz left the theatre, until the moment she was pulled from the cab.

He did his best to reassure her that Roz would be found. She was obviously distressed by the lack of news about her friend. Afraid that something bad might have happened to her. She was not alone in that, he thought.

Putting down the phone he went over everything she had told him. One of the things the cabbie had said to her stuck in his mind. Before pulling her from the cab he had told her he wasn't interested in her. To Ballinger, this confirmed his fears that this was all was about Roz.

He left the house. Moved into the barn. He needed to keep himself busy, so he began working on the Discovery.

He began fitting the replacement windscreen and new tailgate window, both of which had arrived while he was in London. Once these tasks were completed, he began work on plugging the bullet holes in the bodywork.

When this was done, he took off his coveralls, locked the barn, and returned to the house. He scrubbed his hands, washed his face, then slipped into his jacket, ready to nip across to the pub for lunch.

The phone rang. It was DI Meadowcroft.

'You just caught me!' he told the policeman. 'I was on my way out to lunch.'

'I won't keep you long. I thought you'd like an update. We've ruled out your Shogun friend,' he said. 'We have video showing the two girls being picked up by a bogus taxicab. Seems this bloke has been picking up women all over the South East, and then raping them.'

'Then what does he do with them?' asked Ballinger.

'Usually, he lets them go.'

'Has he let Roz go?'

'Not yet.'

'Why not?'

'We don't know.'

'I do,' Ballinger told him. 'I don't believe this was just a random abduction. I think this was about Roz. I think your cabbie was paid to abduct her, and he has now passed her on to whoever he was working for.'

'You have evidence supporting this?'

'Only what he said.'

'What he said?'

'He told Charlie he wasn't interested in her.'

'Come on, Ballinger, that could mean anything. Perhaps she simply wasn't his type.'

'Cobblers! What kind of rapist would abduct two victims, and then keep one and let the other one go?'

'This is a man driven by sexual fantasies, Ballinger. He's not going to act in any logical manner. Look, I know you think someone is out to harm her, and I understand that you feel partly responsible for what happened to her. But there is no evidence to suggest that this is anything other than an abduction for sexual gratification.

Now, I have put out an alert on your Shogun friend, just in case. But for now there is nothing more we can do about him. I'm sorry, but that's the way it is,' and with that, the policeman ended the call.

Ballinger had lost his appetite. If he was right, and he was convinced he was, then Roz was now in the hands of a killer, or killers. Even if he was wrong, she was still in a world of trouble and, as Meadowcroft had so rightly pointed out, he felt wholly responsible for this.

Forgetting lunch, he walked down the lane to the farm. Beside the main hay barn stood two small transport containers. Ballinger rented one of the containers from the farmer, as an overspill storage unit for motor parts. As he was unlocking the container the farmer came out of the barn. He nodded a greeting.

'You hear all the shooting the other night?' he asked.

'Someone in the back field,' Ballinger told him. 'They legged it when I went out there.'

'Bloody lunatics,' grumbled the farmer. 'Firing off guns in the dark. I'll be on to the police if they do it again.'

Entering the container, Ballinger collected together all the things he needed to finish off the bodywork repairs. Dropped them into a cardboard box.

Moving to the back of the container he unlocked a rusting filing cabinet that stood in the corner. He pulled open the bottom drawer and, from behind it, lifted out the zip bag containing his Glock. Adding it to the box, he left the container, locked it up, and carried everything back to the house.

He put the Glock in the gun cupboard and headed back to the workshop. Set to work on the plugs he had inserted. He rubbed them down until they were as smooth as he was ever going to get them, then carefully sprayed them with primer. When the primer had set, he applied the first topcoat and set up the drying lamps.

Restoring cars was a labour of love for Ballinger. It also helped take his mind off more serious concerns. By the end of the day he had succeeded in forgetting his troubles for a short while, and the Discovery was back to its usual, pristine, condition. But the sense of satisfaction he usually felt was dulled, by a heavy sense of foreboding.

Later he sat in the kitchen drinking his nightcap. Another day, and still no word. It was driving him crazy, having to carry on as though everything was alright when it so plainly was not. But what could he do? He was totally out of options.

He thought again about the break-in on the night he had stayed over at McKay's place. He could not for one minute believe that his former comrade would betray him. Yet, neither could he believe that someone had followed him all the way to Cumbria that day, via Belfast and Manchester.

The only other possibility that came to mind was that Dawson had asked the phone company to ping his phone, and check on his whereabouts that night? Not something they would normally agree to do without official sanction. But he could not discount the possibility that the one-time agent might have had friends with that kind of clout.

He stared morosely into his whisky-glass. Once again, he found himself sitting here at the end of a long, and fruitless, day. Still with more questions going around in his head than he had answers for.

49

Sunday Week 3

Eight-o-clock the next morning, and his phone was ringing. He recognised the Newton Stewart area code. It was David Moss.

'Go to your computer!' the retired newspaper reporter told Ballinger. 'I have something for you.'

Ballinger went into the study. He opened his laptop. 'Okay,' he told Moss when it had booted up.

'Check out the Sunday Observer's article on Dawson.'

Ballinger opened up the Observer. Two days ago, the murder of an ex-intelligence officer in his own home was headline news. Now the story had been relegated to the inside second page.

He studied the article. It was not quite an obituary, more a resume of Dawson's career in the service of his country. The piece incorporated a grainy photograph that he recognised at once. It was a copy of the framed photograph he had seen on the window sill, inside Dawson's apartment.'

'Found it?' asked Moss.

'I've found it.'

'D'you see the picture?'

'Yes.'

'That's Dawson and his wife. According to this article

she died from cancer three years ago. Can you believe it, I actually knew that woman? She was a Newton Stewart girl. Her parents ran a small bakery here. From what I remember, she left around the time of the millennium. Went south to work in London.'

'That is one hell of a coincidence,' voiced Ballinger.

'You think so, do you? Well I haven't finished yet. See the big house in the picture, behind them? That's Hugh McDonald's place. I couldn't believe it when I saw it. What the hell were Dawson and his wife doing, paying a social visit to McDonald.

'I don't know,' growled Ballinger. 'But I am going to find out. Where is this place?' Dunn gave Ballinger directions to McDonald's house.

'I hope you are going to keep in the loop about what's going on,' said the Scot.

'I'll do that,' promised Ballinger. He thanked Moss then rang off. Taking a photo of the on-screen image, he sent the shot to Dutton. Then called his number.

'I've sent you a picture. Take a look.'

Dutton opened up the photo. 'Who is it?' he asked.

'That's Gerald Dawson and his wife. Turns out she was from Newton Stewart.'

'That's interesting!'

'Guess who the house belongs to?'

'Go on?'

'Retired Brigadier, Hugh McDonald.'

'The guy who owns the Loch?'

'The same.'

'Looks like they're there on holiday?'

'That's what I thought.'

'Someone needs to have a chat with the Brigadier?'

'Just what I was thinking.'

'Where is Mrs Dawson now?' asked Dutton.

'She died, some time back.'

'Well if McDonald *is* involved with Dawson, he might just know who was in that car that was pulled from his loch. He might even know where Roz is?'

'I'm not holding my breath on that. But he has to be worth questioning. And anything is better than sitting around here, doing nothing.'

'Tell me about it,' sighed Dutton.

'Any luck with those passenger lists?' asked Ballinger.

'Yes and no. Fancy a trip to Sweden?'

'Sweden?'

'Gothenburg! It's where Stena's head office is based. Where they keep their records.'

'Oh, I see! Well, let's see what this trip to Scotland brings first, shall we. Then we'll talk about that.'

'Okay! Take care up there,' Dutton told him.

50

Using the motorbike, Ballinger cut the journey time to six and a half hours. At a little before four-o-clock he rode up the narrow, winding, lane leading to the home of Hugh McDonald.

The lane ended at an open, cobbled, courtyard that extended the whole way around the large, stone, house. To the left of the house stood a garage that once might have been a coach house. To the right, a gateway with no gate.

The place had seen better days. Dark moss grew wildly in the crevices between the granite stones of the house. The same moss permeated the gaps between the badly worn cobblestones. Elsewhere, a spreading assortment of weeds covered the ground.

Riding through the gateway to the back of the house, he switched off the ignition. He removed the helmet, goggles, and his gauntlets, and pulled on a pair of transparent surgical gloves. He opened the pannier and took out the gun. Unzipping his leather jacket, he slipped the gun into the holster.

The noise of the bike would have alerted McDonald to his arrival. Ballinger didn't care. He was finished with knocking on doors. He would deal with the Brigadier if, and when, he came out to investigate.

He was in an old stable yard. He entered the nearest stable and looked inside. There was no place to conceal anyone in there. He checked the other stables. They were all empty. He made for the back door of the house. It was not locked.

Pulling the gun, he stepped into a kitchen that looked like something from a nineteen-forties, wartime movie. It took him less than a minute to establish there was no one on the ground floor.

He climbed the stairs. There was no one in any of the four bedrooms. Nor in the antiquated bathroom that served them all.

Back on the landing he spotted a small trapdoor that gave access to the loft. Going downstairs he took a set of step ladders from the cubby hole beneath the staircase. Carried them up to the landing.

Opening the step ladders he climbed up. Pushed the trapdoor aside, then climbed onto the top step. With his phone on torch, he shone it around the roof space.

The place was cavernous. Dark corners and gloomy areas stretched away to where the light from his torch could not reach. Every inch of the place was covered by a thick, even, layer of black dust. No one could have gone up there without causing major disturbance to the dust and there was no indication of that. He mentally wrote off the loft as a place of concealment.

Closing the trap door, he returned the steps to their niche below the stairs then went back outside the house. He approached the garage. Gripping the Glock, he pulled open the side access door.

In the centre of the garage stood the old Volvo. Brigadier Hugh McDonald sat in the front passenger seat with a shotgun between his knees. There was a great hole, where the back of his head should have been.

Ballinger opened the car door. He studied the gun. It was a 12 bore, long barrelled, antique Purdy. He very much doubted the man had killed himself using that. If McDonald had placed the business end of this gun barrel into his mouth, as he appeared to have done, it was unlikely he would have been able to reach the trigger.

Carefully he checked the interior of the car and then the boot. There was no sign of anyone having been concealed in either.

Heading back to the house it occurred to him that a place this size ought to have a cellar. He found the entrance around the other side of the house, guarded by a locked door. Returning to the kitchen he removed the bunch of keys hanging from the back of the door. One of them fitted the cellar door and he pulled it open.

Using the torch he went down the stairs, into a small wine cellar. There were sundry pieces of junk stored down there, including an old set of golf clubs. But there was no wine. No Roz Carroll, either.

Back in the house he began a more comprehensive search of the place. He didn't know what he was looking for, but right now he'd settle for anything.

Starting upstairs he checked out the three unused bedrooms. Their empty wardrobes and drawers told him nothing.

McDonald's room was a little more productive. Lying under some bedsheets, in a chest of drawers, he found an old Browning revolver and its holster. Ballinger took out the gun. It was part loaded. He put his nose to the barrel. The gun had been fired recently.

Putting the weapon back in the drawer he finished his search of the room. Finding nothing more, he moved downstairs. Began checking the dining room and lounge, rifling through cupboards and drawers. It took him twenty minutes to find, precisely, nothing. With a growing sense of hopelessness he moved on to the kitchen.

Ten minutes later with his search complete, Ballinger sat at the kitchen table. He took a small swig from the half empty bottle of whiskey he had discovered in the kitchen cabinet. Allowed the liquid to roll around his mouth, and then let it slide, smoothly, down his throat.

He recapped the bottle and regarded it, pensively. Suddenly he exploded with anger. 'Shit!' he swore. 'Shit! Shit! Shit!' He hurled the bottle across the kitchen. It hit the wall above the ancient cooker and shattered, spreading whiskey and glass fragments everywhere.

Within seconds the rage had passed off. He grinned ruefully. Slightly embarrassed by his own outburst. Pulling out his phone he called Dutton. Told him what he had found in Newton Stewart. More importantly, what he had not found.

'You need to get out of there,' Dutton told him. 'Before someone turns up. You've done all you can. We'll just have to hope the police can find her.'

'I'm not holding my breath, there,' voiced Ballinger. 'Last I heard, they were chasing phantom taxi drivers. Listen, Terry,' he told his friend, 'I'm calling in on Colin McKay on my way back. See what he has to say for himself. I'll call you from there before I leave.'

'I'm not going anywhere,' he was told.

Ballinger ended the call and put the phone in his pocket.

51

Ballinger rode down the busy road. After crossing the border at Gretna, he had remained on the M6 only as far as junction 44. From there he cut across country towards Cockermouth. Then picked up the A66 Keswick road.

Soon he found himself following the contours of the lake. This time approaching the house from the opposite direction. Just before the entrance to McKay's place he pulled off the road. Taking out his phone he composed a text to Dutton. Read it through, then pressed send.

Just here, the trees between the road and the water formed a dense copse. He waited until there was a lull in traffic then turned the bike onto a foot trail. Fifty yards in, he stopped and dismounted.

Leaving the trail, he wheeled the bike into the trees. Pushed it deep into a thick clump of undergrowth where it would not be seen. He stripped off his leathers, rolled them up, and left them with the bike. Then, gun in hand, he set off through the trees.

He would have preferred to have waited until nightfall. But by then it might be too late – if it wasn't already too late. He checked the time. Six-forty. He moved faster, angling towards the lake. Soon he began to catch glimpses of water through the trees, its surface glittering in the evening sunlight.

After five minutes he came to a wide, pebbled, pathway that had been cut through the trees. A quick glance showed the path ran from the side of McKay's house, to a small wooden boathouse by the water's edge.

Staying behind the tree line he worked his way down to the boathouse. The door was secured by a padlock. Using his knife as a lever he wrenched off the hasp and stepped inside.

A narrow jetty ran out into the lake. A fourteen-foot cuddy boat was moored to the jetty. The cuddy cabin ran from the vessel's prow, to the mid-section. It had no door. Just a curtain hanging across the entrance. A bench seat ran across the stern. Behind the seat, a retractable outboard motor was mounted on the transom.

Stepping onto the boat he quickly checked the low cabin. It was empty. He climbed back up onto the jetty and exited the small building. He was pushing the door shut when he heard a voice he knew well.

'Don't turn around, Sandy. Stay right where you are, or I'll put a bullet in your back.'

Ballinger stood stock still. 'Good of you to confirm what I thought, Col,' he voiced. 'Saved me the trouble of having to beat it out of you.'

'Shut up, Sandy. Now, very slowly, take hold of the gun by the barrel and lift it up as high as you can. Make sure you keep it where I can see it, or I might just panic and shoot you. Go on, lift it up.'

Fuming at his own carelessness Ballinger took hold of the gun barrel and slowly lifted it high.

'Okay, now throw it out into the water, as far as you can. Don't try any heroics or you'll be dead before you even get the chance to turn round.

Ballinger swung his arm and threw the Glock out into the lake.

'Now the knife! And your phone!'

He reached down. Removed the knife from its ankle sheath and tossed it into the water, followed by his phone.

'Now spread your feet, get the palms of your hands up on the door, and stay like that. You know how this works. You've done it to others, often enough.'

He did as he was told. Footsteps approached him from behind. Then, without warning, something came down onto the back of his head and the world went black.

Ballinger opened his eyes. He was bound to a heavy wooden chair in McKay's lounge. Sitting opposite him, in his favourite armchair, was Colin McKay. 'How's the head?' he asked.'

'Like you care,' voiced Ballinger. 'How's the girl?'

'She's okay,' McKay told him.

'She'd better be.'

'Saw you coming a mile off, Sandy. Got no end of motion sensors and hidden cameras dotted around this place. All courtesy of Gerry Dawson's clever boys.'

Ballinger said nothing.

'How long have you known?' asked McKay.

'Not long. My house was broken into, the night I stayed here,' Ballinger told him. 'Apart from myself, you were the only person who knew I would away from home, so it did cross my mind you might be involved. But I never gave it any serious consideration. I thought, perhaps, my phone was being tracked.'

'Well that was Dawson for you. He told me you'd never even know someone had been in your house.'

'Perhaps his 'boys' are not that clever,' said Ballinger. 'But then, neither are you. I just found half a bottle of your favourite tipple in McDonald's kitchen cabinet. I knew it couldn't be his. No true Scot would drink Irish. So I thought, who do I know who drinks Bushmills sixteen-year-old malt whiskey, and doesn't live a million miles from Newton Stewart?'

'Well, there you go,' smiled McKay. 'My mother always said that drinking would get me into trouble. What were you doing at Mac's place, anyway?'

'There's a picture of Dawson and his wife in the Observer. Standing in front of McDonalds house.'

McKay nodded. 'It's his father's house - or was.'

'Sorry?'

'Mac, and Gerry. They were father and son.'

'Really?'

'Mac once worked out of the Defence Ministry, in London,' explained McKay. 'He had a fling with this civilian clerk, Marjorie Dawson she was called, and put her up the duff. Of course, by the time Gerry was born Mac was long gone.

When Marjorie died, Gerry went looking for his father. Managed to track him down. Strangely enough, for two such arrogant bastards, they got on really well together. And Mac proved quite useful, with his loch.'

'So useful you killed him?'

'He killed himself, Sandy. Surely you saw that?'

'Yeah, right!' Ballinger studied his former friend. 'So, why take the girl, Col? She doesn't know anything.'

'I needed bait. To reel you in. She should have gone up to Mac's place, but the old man got cold feet and refused to have her.'

'Is that why you killed him? Because he wouldn't go along with your plan?'

'It was Gerry's plan. Not mine. But no, that is not why I killed him. Mac knew far too much for anyone's comfort. He should have been put down years ago. But with Gerry around, that was never going to happen.

In the end I decided to get rid of them both. I shot Gerry with his father's gun, then slipped it back into the old man's bedroom drawer.' He smiled. 'Beautiful, isn't it? Man shoots his son, then kills himself.

'How did you find out where Roz was?'

'Facebook. Where else? She's been giving a running commentary on her time in London. She even told everyone she was going to the theatre that night, to see Wicked. Made it easy for us. But then, so did you. Here I was, all ready to set a trap for you, and you just walk right in.' McKay knocked back the whiskey he was nursing. He looked at Ballinger. 'I dare say you've worked it all out?'

'More or less. Maguire killed Carroll and dumped him in the loch. Then took his identity so that he could start a new life, using Carroll's name and the money he had stolen. I assume it was Dawson who ferried him down to Dorset. I'm just not quite sure where you fitted in.'

'Maguire approached me for help when he decided to do a runner,' explained McKay. 'I set up the Irish end of things. Arranged for him and Carroll to be on the same ferry. Carroll thought he was getting a lift to Aberdeen, to start a new job on an oil rig. But the job never existed. He only got as far as the loch. The rest of the arrangements were down to Gerry. It was his idea to use his father's fishing loch.'

'I take it the car was always meant to be found?'

McKay nodded. 'It was! It just took longer than we thought. Not that it mattered, Gerry had the investigation moved to London. He sent off hair samples from the real Joseph Maguire, alias Michael Carroll, to the Northern Ireland Police Service. Their DNA was checked against that of Maguire's brother, and they matched. Maguire was declared dead. We were home and dry.'

'So why did you give me Maguire's name when I came to you?'

'I had no choice, Sandy. His name would have popped up the minute you started digging. He was always the most obvious candidate. If I hadn't mentioned him, you'd have wondered why I hadn't. Besides, I needed to buy some time so I could tie up the rest of the loose ends – of which you are one. Sorry, but you really have brought this upon yourself.'

52

Each time she awoke they gave her food and water. When she had eaten and drank, and used the en suite toilet in the room, her wrists and feet were again bound to the bed rails and she was put back to sleep.

She didn't know how long she had been in this place. It was daylight when she arrived, daylight each time she was awakened. She thought there were just two men in the house. The driver, and the one who seemed to be in charge. But it was always the driver who woke her up.

He was here now. Watching her. Perched on the chair, as always, between her and the bedroom door. But today something had changed. Today she had not been given anything to eat, or drink. She wondered why this was, but she was afraid to ask. She risked a glance at the man she had come to regard as her jailer.

'How's your neck?' she asked, remembering the blow she had given him. She liked to wind him up. It was the only weapon she had. Normally he ignored her jibes. This time, surprisingly, he came back at her.

'You think you are one clever little bitch, don't you?' he told her. 'Well let me tell you where being clever can get you, sweetheart. Your old man was clever. Very clever. In fact, he was so clever it got him killed. Along with your mammy and your brother.'

His words fell like hammer blows. They took her breath away. She almost choked on the rush of bile that filled her mouth. She turned away so he couldn't see how much he had hurt her. Fighting back tears she forced herself to climb from the bed. She walked like an automaton into the toilet and closed the door. Once inside, she broke down, completely.

'Not such a clever bitch now, are you?' she heard him call after her.

After a while she pulled herself together. The last thing she wanted was for him to follow her into the toilet to see what she was doing. She washed her hands then swilled her face with cold water. Studied herself in the mirror.

Yellow bruising covered her cheek where the back of his hand had struck. The bruise was leeching towards her right eye, and she worried she might end up with a shiner. Then she reminded herself that she had bigger things to worry about than a black eye.

So, her mother, brother, and father really were dead, if this man was to be believed. She had often wondered how she would feel upon receiving this news. Vindication, perhaps, of her own, long held, view? Closure of a sort? She felt neither. Just a deep, hollow, void of sadness.

Leaving the bathroom, she returned to the bed. She looked away as he re-tied her bonds. She really didn't want to look at him. Nor speak to him, again. But the need to know overwhelmed all other resolves. 'Did they suffer?' she asked, quietly.

Her captor looked at her. 'No! They were crapping themselves, but in the end, it was quick.'

'Was it you?'

The man nodded.

'Why?'

He seemed to think about this. Then he shrugged. 'It was a mistake.'

A mistake? She closed her eyes. In all the dreams and scenarios her mind had created concerning the fate of her family, never had it entertained the possibility that they had died by some terrible mistake. How could that be?

She felt a sharp sting as the needle entered her arm. She opened her eyes. Seeing her looking, the man put a hand in his pocket and pulled out an object. Holding it up he let the ankh dangle on its chain.

'You should be more careful,' he said. 'You could have lost this. I found it outside. On the path.' He looped the necklace over her head, his eyes laughing at her.

'I don't believe you,' she told him.

'You don't believe what?'

'That you could kill three people by mistake.'

'I didn't say I killed them by mistake. I meant to kill them. The mistake was them being there in the first place, because they shouldn't have been. But that was not my fault. That was down to your clever daddy. It was him who got them killed. *His* mistake, not mine.'

'What do you mean?' she asked. 'Please! I have to know.'

He gave a slight shrug. Began to talk. Later, when he had finished talking, he pushed down the plunger on the syringe, putting her to sleep for the last time.

53

'**So what happened** to Carroll, and his family?' asked Ballinger. 'Did he know too much, too?'

'That was nothing to do with us,' McKay told him. 'In fact, it gave us one hell of a scare. We thought one of the paramilitaries had rumbled us. Taken out Maguire in revenge for stealing their money. Then, to make matters worse, we suddenly had the police threatening to delve into Carroll's background. We couldn't have that. Who knows what they might have found?'

'You mean, like him being left-handed, for one thing,' said Ballinger. 'Gay, for another.'

'Is that right? Well, haven't you been a busy fellow? We hadn't realised he was either. But it goes to prove my point, doesn't it? Those are just the sort of things we couldn't risk coming out.'

'So, Dawson stepped in again,' speculated Ballinger. 'Shut down any potential police investigation into Carroll's background.'

'He was good at that sort of thing. And who's going to argue with the head of the Northern Ireland desk?

'But then Terry Dutton started digging around?'

'I didn't know anything about that, at first,' stated McKay. 'Gerry didn't tell me. He thought he could contain it.'

'By having Dutton run down?'

'Well that's the sort of game they play where he grew up, isn't it? But in fairness, it might have worked. Until you turned up. This was the last thing anybody expected. As soon as I heard your name, I knew we were in trouble.

I told Gerry to start shutting everything down, but he wouldn't. He said he had a good life here. He wasn't prepared to give it up. So he came up with a plan. He was going to have you arrested by the police.'

'He tried,' nodded Ballinger.

'I know. When that didn't work, he borrowed a few trinkets from Shaw's place to hide on your property. He was going to tip off the police again, but by this time I'd had enough of his silly games.'

'So you killed the Shaws, knowing the finger would be pointed at me. Did you kill Badell, too?'

'Badell was a leech. He'd been sponging off Gerry for years. During the police investigation into the Carroll disappearance, he was Gerry's inside man. It was he who gave Gerry the nod that Rudman was about to start looking into Carroll's Irish background. Gave us the chance to put the blockers on.

After Badell had his accident, Gerry bankrolled his bike repair business. He never told me why, but I suspect the little shit had been putting some pressure on him. Threatening to go public about his role in obstructing the original enquiry. If I'd had my way, he'd have been put down there and then. Gerry was too soft in the head.

Anyway, after Gerry failed to get you out of the way, I decided I needed step in and take control. We'd had a good run, but it was time to call it a day and move on. That meant getting rid of you, your friend Dutton, and anyone else who knew anything that might point a finger in my direction.

With the Shaws, I hoped to kill two birds with one stone. Get rid of them and have you put away for their murder. After we put the Shaws down we went after Badel. Made that one look like an accident. *Job done,* I thought. But no! You managed to wriggle out of being arrested again. You really should have let them send you to prison.'

'But why kill the Shaws in the first place? What had they done to deserve that?'

McKay sighed. 'This whole thing was about money. When Maguire did his first disappearing trick, he was sitting on a little under six million pounds. All stashed away in an offshore account. The deal was that, in return for a three-way split, Gerry and I would help him set up a new life on the mainland.

So, Maguire opened up three new accounts in the Caymans, with three equal amounts in each. The first account was in his new name, Michael Carroll. The other two were in mine, and Gerry's.

But the bastard put one over on us. He added his own name to each of our accounts, as a ghost account holder. This meant that every time we drew on our accounts, unbeknown to us he had to countersign the transaction.

I have no idea why he did this? Perhaps he thought we might try to get rid of him, and it was his way of making sure we couldn't. In the event, however, it made little difference to us. Our money was always there when we asked for it.'

'Until he disappeared again,' voiced Ballinger, seeing where this was going.

'Until he disappeared! Then, the next time Gerry tried to draw some money the bank refused to release it. When he asked them why, he was shown how the accounts had been set up. Told that unless the bank received Carrol's countersignature, which was never going to happen, they could not release the funds.

Gerry and I came up with a plan. We told the bank that Carroll was dead. Thought this might be enough to unlock our accounts. But it didn't work. They wanted to see a copy of his death certificate which, since nobody knew whether he was dead or alive, was also never going to happen. So, there we were, up the creek.

Then, enter Frank Shaw. It was Gerry who found him. Shaw was a County registrar. He was also a greedy bastard who, for fifty grand, was prepared to issue a bone fide death certificate in the name of Michael Thomas Carroll.

As part of the deal, Gerry took up the lease on the Carroll house and put the Shaws in there, rent free. Shaw got his money and a nice house to live in. We got a genuine death certificate, and access to our money.'

Just then the door behind Ballinger swung open. Someone with a heavy tread entered the room.

'How's it going?' asked a voice.

54

'I hate waiting around,' Grumbled Dutton, as he and Alex returned to their room from dinner.

'What time did he say he'd call?' asked Alex.

'He didn't! He just said he was looking in on Colin Mckay, and he'd give me a call, when he left.'

'Who's Colin McKay?'

'Someone he used to work with in Northern Ireland. Sandy thought he might be able to help us.'

'And did he?'

'Not really! In fact, I don't think Sandy trusts him too much now. Last week he went to the Lake District to see McKay and stayed the night. While he was there someone broke into his house, and McKay was the only person who knew he was away from home, that night.'

'Does he think McKay is involved?'

'Has to be a possibility. He's probably calling there to tackle him about it. The mood he's in, he's going to be asking McKay some pretty serious questions.'

'Is he dangerous, this McKay?'

Dutton thought about this. 'I think most of the people he used to know are dangerous,'

'Then he could be walking into trouble.'

He nodded. 'He could. But I'm sure he'll have thought about that. He usually knows what he's doing.'

Dutton checked his watch. 'It was about five-o-clock when he called from McDonald's house. It's now almost seven. I'll give him another half hour. Then if I haven't heard anything, I'll give him a call.'

55

Ballinger turned his head as the newcomer stepped into view. He was big. Strong. Somewhere in his fifties, with cropped, greying hair. 'Mister fixit, I presume?' he addressed the newcomer.

'How's the car?' asked the man.

'It's sorted. Why did you run off?'

'Too much gunfire,' shrugged the man. 'I thought it might bring the people out from the farm. Also, I had to collect the girl.'

'Is she asleep?' McKay asked the stranger.

The man nodded.

Ballinger looked at McKay. 'Where did you find Rambo, here?'

'This is Brendan,' announced McKay. 'Brendan Craig. Back in '97 Brendan was sent down for shooting two armoured car, security guards. While he was locked away his girlfriend and his sons were killed when her car was hit by a truck, driven by Michael Carroll. It was an accident, but that didn't make them any less dead, did it, Brendan?'

'That bastard killed my family,' spoke up the man. 'He had no right to live.'

McKay continued. 'When Brendan was released in 2012, he began looking for Carroll. It took him a while, but he found him. Or thought he had.'

'He though Maguire was Carroll?' asked Ballinger.

'I didn't know?' shrugged the big man. 'How would I? He was calling himself Carroll. I called at the house in the middle of the night. I was dressed as a policeman. All three of them came downstairs. They thought something had happened to the girl.

It was like lambs to the slaughter. When I told Carroll what I was doing, and why, he started to talk, and Jesus did he talk. It all came out. Who he really was, where he was from, how he had ended up in Dorchester. He had to be telling the truth. No one comes up with a story like that out of nowhere.'

'But you killed them anyway,' said Ballinger, drily.

'So what was I supposed to do? Say sorry! Give them a bag of sweeties, and a ride home?'

'Where are they?' asked Ballinger.

'Same place I left the Shaws. I dropped them down a shaft in the basement.

McKay took up the story. 'When interest in the family's disappearance died down, Brendan contacted Gerry. He wasn't greedy. He just wanted a steady, well paid, job. So Gerry put him on his Company's payroll as a sort of odd job man.'

Ballinger studied his former colleague 'Why have you done this, Col? Okay, Dawson was always a piece of shit, I get that, but not you. What happened to bring you to this?'

'The winds of change happened Sandy. It seemed there was to be no place for people like me in the new Ulster. We were an embarrassment. A relic of the old order. All those years fighting the bombers, the snipers, the killers of innocent people, suddenly meant nothing. It was *Thanks mucker, now away and fuck off.* That's what I got for my contribution to keeping the peace.

So when Maguire came along, I decided to buy myself a future. I knew Gerry Dawson would be up for it, so I signed him up. Together we set it all up.

We've had a good thing going, these past few years. Now, thanks to you and your friend Dutton, it's all gone, and a lot of people are dead.'

McKay turned to his accomplice. 'Okay, Brendon, I'm going to ask my friend here a few questions now,' he said. 'Why don't you show him what will happen if I don't think he is answering truthfully.'

Craig grinned. He put his hand in his pocket and pulled out a cigarette lighter. He flicked it on then turned up the flame until it was like a mini blowtorch.

Stepping behind the chair he applied the flame to a small area at the base of Ballinger's skull. There was a crackling noise and the smell of burning hair, followed by white hot pain. Ballinger cried out. He threw his head forward to get away from the heat. McKay nodded, and the lighter was shut down.

'Just a little demonstration, Sandy. I'm sure it won't be necessary. So, just to set the record straight, besides your friend Dutton – and I'll take it as read that he knows everything you do – who else knows the truth about Carroll?

'Nobody. We kept it all in house. Most of what we had was speculation, anyway. Until today.'

'What about the police?'

'You mean Penny? He doesn't know anything.'

'I don't believe that. He must have given you a hard time about the Shaws. What did you tell him?'

'I told him nothing. I didn't need to. I'd removed the stolen items your friends had left, and I was nowhere near Dorchester when they were killed.'

'What about the Met?'

'I told them we were looking into the Carroll disappearance. I had no choice. It was obviously linked to the abduction, and they needed as much information as I could give them. I also mentioned the deaths back in Dorset. Told them they, too, might be linked.'

'How did they take that?'

'Said it sounded like a paperback novel.'

'Did you give them my name?'

'Why would I? I thought you were a friend?'

'What does Dutton know about me?'

'He knows I came up here to see you last week, that's all. He just has you down as a possible source of information.'

'Does he know you are here now?'

'No. I told him I was heading home.'

'When did you tell him that?'

'Just before I left McDonald's place.

'Why would you tell him you were going home if you intended to come here?'

Ballinger shrugged. 'He's an ex-copper. He likes to do things by the book. If I told him I suspected you were involved, he would have called it in to his friends. The cavalry would have been here by now.'

'So you wanted to be the hero, is that it? Come here and save the girl yourself?'

'Not really. I just didn't want the police involved. They don't have the best of records when it comes to rescuing kidnap victims, do they?'

'They don't,' voiced McKay. 'But then neither do you, if today's performance is anything to go by. So where is he now, your friend Dutton?'

'He's in Norfolk. Staying at a health club.'

'Which one?'

'I don't know, I didn't book it.'

'Where is it?'

'Somewhere near Kings Lynn.'

McKay nodded at Craig. The lighter was flicked on. Again, the searing pain at the back of his head made Ballinger gasp.

'Where is he, Sandy?'

'I don't know,' insisted Ballinger. His wife booked the place. Why would I need to ask where they were staying? If I need him, I can call him.'

McKay looked thoughtfully at Ballinger. Then gave a careless shrug.

'No matter. A few phone calls will tell us where he is. I just needed to know that no one was about to come knocking on my door in the next few hours. Asking embarrassing questions. I hope they don't, Sandy, because if they do, the girl will be the first to die. And then you.'

Ballinger shrugged. 'There's no one I know, likely to be coming here. But the police are looking for the girl. Who knows where they are up to? They could be creeping up on this place as we speak.'

McKay smiled. 'I'll take my chances with the Met. They can't see anything beyond Watford.'

'Come on, Col,' pleaded Ballinger. 'Let the girl go. She can't harm you. She doesn't know a thing.'

'She knows I killed her family,' spoke up Craig. He shrugged. 'She did ask.'

McKay climbed to his feet. 'Okay, put him out,' he instructed his accomplice. 'Make sure you give him plenty. It doesn't matter if he overdoses. As long as he doesn't come round.'

Craig took the box from his pocket. Opened it up. 'There's only one left,' he told McKay.

'Then get the other box!'

Craig shook his head. 'It's not here! We gave it to McDonald, remember, to use on the girl.'

'Then just give him what you have,' instructed McKay. 'If he starts to come round, we'll shoot him.'

As Craig prepared the drug, Ballinger struggled to free himself. He quickly realised he was wasting his time. He tried a different approach. 'You know he'll kill you as soon as you've helped him get rid of everyone else,' he told Craig. 'You'll be just another loose end. Like the rest of us.'

'Save your breath,' McKay told him. 'Brendan and I have plans. We will be starting new lives, in new places, courtesy of the new passports Gerry supplied. You'll settle for that, won't you Craig?'

The big man nodded. Ballinger watched helplessly as the needle was plunged into his arm. With a smile of real pleasure Craig depressed the plunger. Within seconds his world spun away into nothing.

56

Dutton checked his watch again. It was now after seven-thirty, and still no word from Ballinger. He picked up the phone to call him and noticed the flashing icon.

'Alex, there's a message on here, from Sandy!' He opened it up. '*McKay gone bad. If I haven't called you in the next hour, send in your friends.*' He showed the message to Alex.

'When did that come in?' she asked.

'Six-thirty. We were having dinner. I left the phone up here, didn't I.'

'What does it mean?'

'It means he's in trouble. See if you can find the number for the Cumbria police, will you!' He fast-dialled Ballinger's number. It came back unobtainable. He tried again, without success.

Alex held up her own phone to show the number she had found. He tapped it in.

'Cumbria police,' announced the switchboard. Dutton asked for the duty CID officer.

'Can I ask what this is about, sir?'

'I have some information about a kidnapping,' he told her.

Dutton was put through to a Detective Sergeant, called Brookes. Dutton asked if there was someone more senior available. There wasn't.

Keeping it simple, he said who he was then gave out McKay's address. He explained that his associate had gone to the place make some enquiries about a recent kidnapping. That he had failed to call in at his check-in time, and he was concerned about the man's safety.

'What is the name of this associate of yours?'

'Ballinger! John Ballinger.'

'And you are saying that someone is being held against their will in this property.'

'I did not say that. I said that Mr Ballinger was going there to talk to someone who might be involved in a kidnapping. He was supposed to call me back and has not done so. This is out of character, and I am concerned for his safety.'

'Have you tried calling him?'

'I have. His phone is switched off, which again is concerning.'

'Might he be driving?'

'He might. But he always has blue tooth switched on when he drives.'

'Well, we are talking about the Lake District here, sir. There are one or two areas in there with less than full coverage.'

'Sergeant, Mr Ballinger should have contacted me. He has failed to do so. Given that I am unable to raise him, and the nature of his enquiry, I think it might be a good idea for you to take my concerns seriously.'

'I am taking you seriously, sir. I am just exploring other possibilities. Look, why don't you leave this with me, Mr Dutton. I will get someone to look into it.'

'I think, Sergeant, that I would feel so much better if you looked into it yourself.'

'Look, sir, I know you are worried. But I really feel it is a little early to start panicking just yet. I will send a car to check out this address for you, and then call you back. That okay?' and with this the phone went dead.

Dutton closed the phone. He looked at Alex. 'Why do I feel I just wasted five minutes of my life?'

'Why don't you forget the locals, Terry. Call the police in London and tell them what has happened. Tell them Sandy may be in danger. Roz, too, if she is there.'

'Good thinking!' He checked the number Ballinger had given him. Made the call.

'DI Meadowcroft,' said the voice.

Dutton explained who he was. Once more he went through the procedure of telling a police officer about his concerns, and why he was calling.

'Where is this place?' asked Meadowcroft before Dutton had even finished.

'Thornthwaite. In Cumbria.'

'Cumbria? Did you say Cumbria?'

'I did!'

The man swore softly, then spoke urgently. 'Right, Mr Dutton! You'd better give me that address.'

In the Penrith CID duty office, DS Brookes finished typing up the case notes he had been working on before the interruption. This done he set off for the control room. He didn't hurry. This Dutton bloke was almost certainly over-reacting.

As he was about to leave the office, the DCI's phone began to ring. When no one picked it up, the phone on the Inspector's desk began to ring. After a while, it too stopped ringing. He waited a few moments, then moved on. Halfway down the corridor he heard his own desk phone begin to ring. 'Too late, pal,' he grunted. 'I'm busy now.'

He ducked into the small alcove where the coffee machine sat. Drew what the machine laughingly called a Latte. He stood for a while sipping the tasteless, but hot, liquid until he had taken the top off it. Then he continued on his journey.

Carrying the coffee, he entered the stair well. He walked down to the ground floor and pushed through the doors.

Something was going on. Uniforms were scurrying by like their tails were on fire. He followed the crowd into a briefing room that was rapidly filling with bodies.

The room was buzzing. The Superintendent was on the phone, speaking to someone higher up the command chain. The duty Inspector was also on the telephone, pacing up and down and barking out orders.

'What's going on?' Brookes asked a uniform he vaguely knew.

'Big flap on!' she told him. 'The Met have been on. They have a high profile kidnap victim traced to a house over Bassenthwaite. The Super's calling out everybody but the bloody army. Hostage team, shooters, the lot.'

'Oh, bugger,' sighed Brookes.

57

Ballinger was being tossed around in an ocean of syrup. There was something heavy draped across his body and, in the next room, someone was using a jack hammer. To make matters worse, somewhere inside his head a small, but insistent, voice kept telling him he needed to wake up: and he wasn't even asleep.

He lay on his side alternating between periods of semi-wakefulness, and dark spells of dreamless sleep. Each time awareness crept in, the turbulent motion, the weight pinning him down, and the clamouring jack hammer were there. At times, it felt like they had always been there. Then, quite suddenly, it all changed.

The sound of the jack hammer died: the turbulence was quickly reduced to a gentle rocking motion: and the ensuing hush was broken only by the sound of lapping waves.

But even this did not last. New sounds soon reached his ears. Voices. The sound of men grunting, straining, and swearing. Then for one brief, blessed, moment the weight was lifted from his body. Only to crash back down again with painful force.

'Heavy bitch!' complained someone. 'There's no way I can lift her, bent over like this. It'll do my back in.'

'It's all that keep fit stuff they do,' said another voice.

'Some of these girls are more fanatical than the men, so they are. Spend hours in the gym. Okay, so let's forget lifting her. Come this end, and we'll drag her out of here. She won't care.'

'Good thinking!'

Almost at once the weight began to slide away from Ballinger's body, finally fading to nothing.

He opened his eyes. Awake, but unsure where he was. The room in which he lay was dark. What little daylight lay outside the small windows was effectively blocked out by the drawn curtains.

Of the men and their burden, there was no sign. But he could hear them talking. Their voices carried a familiarity that set off alarm bells.

Recognition suddenly kicked in, and his brain snapped back into gear.

He looked around the tiny room. Knew exactly where he was. He was in the cabin on McKay's boat. The jack hammer noise must have been the outboard motor, the weight they dragged off him, Roz. She must have been laid across him in the bottom of the cabin.'

He sat up. His wrists were bound with cable ties, but his feet were not. *Careless*, he thought.

There is a common misconception that cable ties are unbreakable. True, they are next to impossible to break by simply attempting to pull the hands apart. But they can be broken. There is an old escapologist's trick.

Slowly he slid his right foot inward, to raise his knee. Then, lifting his bound hands high he brought them down, hard and fast, across the knee. The force of the impact drove his wrists apart. There was a brief flash of pain as the plastic band bit into his skin, then the sudden, acute, stress inflicted upon the ties caused them to snap at their weakest point, the lugs.

'What was that?' came McKay's voice from outside.

Ballinger rolled back into the position he was lying in when he came round. He feigned unconsciousness. Someone entered the cabin. He tensed himself, ready to spring into action if he had to. A hand rested on his rib cage as someone leaned over him. If the man checked his wrists – '

'Don't mind him,' came the impatient voice of the one called Craig. 'He's not going anywhere, except over the side. Can we get this one sorted first, d'you think?'

There was a grunt from McKay. Then the sound of him scrambling back to the deck. 'You take the top,' instructed Craig. 'One quick lift, and she's gone. Then we can deal with him.'

There was some shuffling around, causing the vessel to rock. Taking advantage of the motion Ballinger climbed to his feet.

'You do know,' went on Craig, conversationally, 'that according to the book, we should slit their bellies before putting them in the water.'

'Stuff the book!' growled McKay. 'There'd be blood everywhere.'

'It stops them bobbing back up to the surface in a day or two.'

'They can bob up all they want! We'll be long gone by then. Let's just throw them over the side, shall we, and get off this fucking boat.'

Craig laughed. 'Not much into sailing, are you? So, why buy a boat if you don't like the water?'

'I didn't buy it. It came with the house.'

Ballinger moved stealthily forward. The cabin roof was so low he had to crouch. A quick glance around offered up nothing he could use as a weapon.

'I think we should have tied their feet,' he heard Craig say. 'We don't want them waking up when they hit the water then trying to swim off. We need them to go straight down.'

The cabin curtain was part open. Through the gap, Ballinger could make out the two men on the deck. Craig was leaning over Roz, his back to the cabin. McKay crouched at the stern, facing forwards.

Carefully Ballinger crept forward, ready to pounce. As he stepped from the darkness of the cabin McKay looked up, and their eyes met. He let out a sharp warning cry.

58

Alerted by the cry, Craig spun around as Ballinger came forward. He charged like a bull, driving his head into Ballinger's stomach. Forcing him back against the cabin.

As the killer came up out of the crouch Ballinger head-butted him in the face, breaking his nose. Craig staggered back, momentarily stunned. Seeing his chance, Ballinger leapt forward. He wrapped his arms around the man's midriff, lifted him off his feet, and swung him, bodily, towards the side of the boat.

Realising what Ballinger was doing, Craig waved his arms around wildly. Searching for anything he could grab hold of to prevent himself being thrown overboard. As his legs came up against the side of the boat, Ballinger released his grip and thrust him away with both hands. Arms still flailing, the big man went down backwards, into the water.

Ballinger had no time to celebrate. A stunning blow caught him in the middle of his back as McKay shoulder-charged him from behind. The blow knocked him completely off balance and, with the boat rocking wildly, he followed Craig over the side.

Diving deeply, he surfaced a few yards away from the vessel. He looked around. Craig was already attempting to pull himself over the gunnel and back into the boat.

Moving rapidly through the water Ballinger leapt onto the killer's back and clung there, his arm wrapped tightly around the Craig's throat, his legs clamped firmly around his thighs, in a scissor hold.

Inside the boat, McKay rushed to help his beleaguered colleague. He reached over to throw a fist at Ballinger's head. The punch went wide and the act of striking out caused McKay to lose his footing. He fell, heavily, against the two struggling men.

The result was disastrous. The combined weight of all three men on the same side of the boat, caused the vessel to keel over. The gunnel dipped below the surface. Water poured onto the boat and rushed into the cabin.

As the vessel tilted Roz's body rolled across the deck, coming to rest against the side of the boat. The vessel tilted even further and Mckay was catapulted, head first, into the water with the others.

Fearing the boat was about to capsize, Craig let go his hold. Falling back into the water he attempted to shake off Ballinger's strong grip.

The sudden release of weight lifted the gunnel clear of the water. But the boat did not right itself. It lay floating on its beam end, the cabin awash.

Ballinger tightened his chokehold on Craigs throat. The man thrashed about like a madman, struggling to break free. With a last desperate effort, the killer managed to plant his feet against the side of the boat. Then, using his lower legs, he thrust his body backwards.

Ballinger was ready for this. Kicking out strongly he absorbed the thrust, taking Craig with him in what was almost a classic life-saving grip. Then he suddenly rolled over so that Craig was face-down in the water.

Holding the man down with the weight of his own body, he released his grip on the killer's throat. Craig, already close to asphyxiation, reacted automatically to his airway being reopened. His lungs expanded rapidly, to gorge on the anticipated, huge, intake of air. They found only water.

Craig's struggles faded as his drowning body began to shut down. Finally just a single hand rose from the water, grasping feebly at the world it had once known. Then it disappeared as the killer's body began its long, slow, descent to the bottom of the lake.

After taking a moment or two to regain his own breath, Ballinger turned his attention to the boat. It lay on its beam ends with the deck rising almost vertically. Fortunately, Roz still lay tucked up against the vessel's side, just clear of the waterline. In the water near the stern, and clinging desperately to the gunnel, was McKay.

'I can't swim,' he voiced fearfully.

'Then now might be a good time to learn,' said Ballinger, impassively,

'Help me Sandy. For old time's sake. Please.'

'You're not my problem,' Ballinger told him. He looked again at the boat. Getting it back of an even keel from the water was impossible. There was only one way out of here for Roz and himself. They were going to have to swim for it. Or rather, he was going to have to swim, with Roz in tow. He moved in close to the vessel.

'What are you doing?' asked McKay.

'I'm taking the girl.'

'What about me?'

'I told you. You're not my problem.'

Reaching in, Ballinger pulled the unconscious girl into

the water and backed away from the vessel, taking her with him. The removal of Roz raised the gunnel an inch or two higher above the surface.

Seeing this, McKay made a desperate attempt to climb back on board. With a sudden lunge he caught hold of the stern bench with his left hand.

'I wouldn't do that!' called out Ballinger.

McKay wasn't listening. Desperate to get out of the water, he pulled himself high enough to get his knees up onto the gunnel. But as he tried to stand, the gunnel dipped once more beneath the surface and the boat began to turn turtle.

With a cry of dismay, McKay fell back into the water. As the boat passed through the perpendicular the outboard motor swung inward and fell from its mounting. Ballinger watched as it crashed down onto McKay's head, driving him below the surface.

The boat came down onto the lake with a huge splash. There it lay, floating, bottom-up and slightly down at the bow. Of McKay, there was no sign.

It was growing dark. Ballinger looked around. In the distance he saw the lights of the traffic, moving along the road beside the lake. Holding onto Roz he began to swim towards them.

A few minutes later she began to stir. Ballinger stopped swimming. Allowed his body to float. Treading water, he wrapped his arms around the girl's waist to keep her head well above the waterline.

Her eyes fluttered open. For a moment she was still. Confused. Unaware of where she was. Then, with a shriek, she exploded into action. Thrashing around in panic as she fought to break free of his grip.

He tightened his hold. She threw her head back. Caught him a stinging blow on the nose that brought tears to his eyes. 'Roz, stop it! It's me, Ballinger. Don't fight me, you'll drown us both. Roz please!'

The message finally got through. She began to calm down. He felt her body relax.

'Is it really you?'

'We've had this conversation before, Roz. Sitting in McDonalds, remember? But don't bother calling me on my phone, to make sure. I seem to have lost it.

'It is you,' she said, relieved. She pulled away from him and he let her go. She turned to face him. 'Bloody hell, it's cold. Where are we?'

'In the middle of a lake. Glad to see you can swim.'

'I'm a good swimmer,' she told him. 'Your nose is bleeding. Did I do that?'

'Don't worry about it.'

'What are we doing in the water?'

'Long story!' he told her. 'But the short answer is, trying to get out. D'you see the traffic back there?' He cocked a thumb back over his shoulder. 'That's the main road. Think you can make it that far?'

She nodded. 'I think so.'

'Then let's go. If you start struggling, give me a shout.' Together, they began swimming for the shore.

Ten minutes later, cold, wet, and not a little weary, they staggered up onto the gently sloping ground beside the lake. Sat there in the evening chill, breathing heavily.

'What happened?' asked Roz at last. 'The last thing I remember was being tied to the bed in that house. That awful man was there.'

'They put us in a boat,' he told her. 'They were going to throw us overboard, but the boat tipped over.'

'How did you get here?' she asked. 'How did you find me?'

'That's another long story. I'll tell you later.'

She looked out across the lake. It was now too dark to make out the upturned boat. 'Where are they?'

'In the water,' he said, simply. 'Don't worry, they won't bother you again. They won't bother anyone again.'

'He said he killed my mum and dad, and Tony.'

'I know.'

'He said he killed them because he thought my dad was someone else. What sort of person does that?'

He had no answer to that. Slowly he climbed to his feet and looked up the road.

'We need to get you somewhere warm,' he told her. 'Think you can make it back to the house?'

'I'm not going back in there.'

'You won't have to if you don't want.'

'Is it far?'

He shook his head. 'It's just up there,' he said, pointing. 'Where all those flashing blue lights are.'

59

A month later.

A blustery wind blew in off the channel. The skies were dark. Filled with grey, threatening, clouds that scudded inland. But so far, the rain had held off. On the isle of Portland the three friends sat in the gazebo, at the back of Dutton's cottage. They were drinking Pinot Noir.

'Roz looked quite the young woman at the funeral,' said Alex. 'Much more mature than her years. I thought she did very well. And I'm glad she decided to have them interred, rather than cremated.'

'I'm not surprised she's aged,' nodded Dutton. 'That business was enough to put years on anyone. But I know what you mean about burials. At least she now knows where her family are, and she'll be able to visit them.' He turned to Ballinger. 'How is she bearing up?'

'Surprisingly well,' observed Ballinger. 'There's a lot of strength in that girl. She certainly doesn't need me riding shotgun for her.'

'I think she sees you as a father figure,' smiled Alex.

'Mister shifter, more like,' he smiled.

Number seven, Mayflower Close, was now on the market. After the funeral of her parents and brother, whose remains had been recovered from a culvert shaft beneath the old mill, Roz had decided to put the house up for sale. Now it had to be cleared of furniture.

Unable to face this task alone, she had called upon Ballinger to help her. She felt that with him nearby, she would be more able to cope. She even offered to pay for his services, but he refused to take anything, saying he was only too happy to help. And he was. He felt the girl would need all the help she could get to put the tragic past behind her and move her life forward again.

Four days ago, for the first time since that fateful day when she had returned from Normandy, Roz Carroll re-entered the house where she had spent so much of her childhood. Ballinger was with her.

'Most of the furniture has gone off to charities,' he remarked. 'But she still has this great stack of things recovered from Council storage and police evidence lockers. Most of it will be thrown out. Some of it she will keep as mementos.

Here's an interesting thing,' he went on. 'Yesterday she showed me a certificate she found. It was issued by the Deed Poll office. It seems that two weeks before he married her mother Maguire changed his name from Joseph Maguire to Michael Thomas Carroll, by fast-track deed poll.'

'That was a hell of a risk to take, wasn't it?' asked Dutton. 'He would have had to show proof of identity in his real name. Anything could have happened?'

'Not as risky as you might think. There must be hundreds of Joseph Maguires in the United Kingdom. Also, the police had stopped looking for the runaway Belfast accountant, hadn't they? They had him down as dead. So the name would not have flagged up any attention.

'Bloody cheeky, though,' voiced Dutton.

'I think he did it for them,' said Alex. 'I think he did it for the woman he was about to marry, and her children.

Think about it. If he had married her, and adopted her children, whilst pretending to be someone else, then both the wedding and the adoptions would have been illegal, and void. So if ever anything happened to him, they would have received nothing from his estate. I think he legally changed his name to protect them.'

'You could be right,' agreed Ballinger. 'Perhaps he did have the odd redeeming quality?'

'Not in my book,' grumbled Dutton. 'He was a thief and a murderer. Always will be.'

'I hope you are not going to keep reminding Roz of that,' commented his wife, drily.

'Ignore him,' grinned Ballinger, 'he can't help it. You know what they say? Once a copper – always a copper.'

End.

Other works by J M Close

INTO THE BLUE

\#

LONG RIDE ON A GHOST TRAIN

Printed in Great Britain
by Amazon